The Six-Gun Syndicate

The Six-Gun Syndicate

X

Norman A. Fox

Thorndike Press • Chivers Press
Thorndike, Maine USA   Bath, England

This Large Print edition is published by Thorndike Press, USA and by Chivers Press, England.

Published in 2000 in the U.S. by arrangement with Richard C. Fox.

Published in 2000 in the U.K. by arrangement with Richard C. Fox.

U.S. Hardcover 0-7862-2422-3 (Thorndike Western Series)
U.K. Hardcover 0-7540-4101-8 (Chivers Large Print)
U.K. Softcover 0-7540-4102-6 (Camden Large Print)

The text of this Large Print edition is unabridged.
Other aspects of the book may vary from the original edition.

Set in 16 pt. Plantin by Al Chase.

Printed in the United States on permanent paper.

British Library Cataloguing-in-Publication Data available

Library of Congress Cataloging-in-Publication Data
Fox, Norman A., 1911–1960.
    The six-gun syndicate / Norman A. Fox.
        p.   cm.
    ISBN 0-7862-2422-3 (lg. print : hc : alk. paper)
    1. Large type books. I. Title.
PS3511.O968 S55 2000
813'.54—dc21   99-089078

The
Six-Gun
Syndicate

one

This was the Bitter Root, land of big mountains and big men, land of sprawling grandeur, magnificent and majestic, and the immensity of it all might have dwarfed that lone rider of the valley trail in spite of the broad shoulders of him. But he was destiny in disguise, a grim purpose personified, and something of the intent that had driven him here seemed to give him a stature beyond measuring.

He had turned his back upon Hamilton at sunup and through all this long day the huddled timber-shrouded hills had paced him in solemn parade and the tang of pine and fir had filled his nostrils. If these were familiar things he gave no indication though he was alert enough, seeing the signs of a dry season, the touch of drought's yellow talons where all should be green and verdant, the haze that hid the heavens yonderly where a forest fire raged in Idaho, over the mountains.

He had come a long ways, this rider, yet for all his apparent interest in his surroundings he might have been a man whose destination lay far beyond him. But as sunset sent the shadow hosts down a dozen mountainsides and those misty minions stole stealthily across Rearing Horse Valley, Battleweed sprawled ahead — trail's end.

He passed the rodeo grounds on the town's ragged outskirts, eyeing the grandstand and bleachers speculatively and with an awakened interest, knowing these were things that had not been here before. He passed a dozen buildings, some old, some new, alike with their false fronts and their wooden awnings, and he dismounted at last before the livery stable to give certain meticulous orders concerning oats and water. Stoop-shouldered Ernie Ide, the hostler, listened with no great interest. But Ernie was old and his eyes were dim and he'd seen too many faces in his time.

Afterwards the stranger angled unerringly to Hop Gow's eating place across the street and his unobtrusive entrance created no commotion. It was past the regular supper hour and the trade had thinned, and the stranger had a booth to himself, where he concentrated on steak and spuds with a seeming disinterest in everything but his plate. If Hop Gow's slanted eyes widened a trifle as he studied the rider, Hop Gow held his heathenish tongue, for twenty years in

Montana had taught that Celestial sage that the ways of white men were beyond understanding and certainly no concern of his.

Fed and rested, the stranger came to the street again, looking contented and almost boyish, a dark-haired, dark-eyed youngster no more than twenty-four. He was not handsome, this stranger, for his features were a trifle too irregular, yet there was something about his lean sun-tanned face that had always made men take a second look and women a third.

His mouth was wide and friendly, his chin rocky and stubborn. Too many trails had flattened his muscles and narrowed his hips, hewing him in the shape of a wedge, and he wore range garb — a gray flannel shirt and a black bandana, brush-scarred levis and scuffed boots — with a careless grace. Smiling he stood there, hip-shot, surveying the street, a leafy tunnel of interlacing cottonwood and elm, almost mellow in the twilight. Then, with no conscious prompting, he headed for the ornate false front of the Buckhorn Saloon.

Thus he walked straight into trouble. It began at the batwings, but that was only a prelude to what followed. It began as the stranger stepped inside, for a gun exploded, the walls hurling back the echo, and his gray

Stetson jerked to sail a score of feet away.

The stranger strode to the hat, moving neither swiftly nor slowly, and picked it up, whistling softly as he eyed the bullet hole drilled through the high crown. Sombrero in place with the brim tugged low, he edged into the saloon again, his right hand brushing a bolstered six-gun at his thigh. This time no one contested his entrance.

The Buckhorn was a place designed for pleasure. Oil paintings of voluptuous ladies, nearly nude, looked down from the walls upon a vast room with tables crowded at its far end — roulette tables, blackjack tables, green-topped and curved, and tables for those who required no other equipment but a deck of cards and a stack of chips. Only a half-dozen men were here and most of these were scattered among the gaming tables. A long bar paralleled one side of the room and a moon-faced barkeep had it to himself. Spread-legged in the center of the open floor, a turbulent island in a sea of sawdust, stood a man with a smoking gun in his hand.

A man? He wasn't more than a boy, this gun-toter, younger even than the stranger, but bigger, much bigger. Blond and ruddy faced, he towered almost to six feet and his blocky body looked just as wide.

"Howdy," he bellowed drunkenly. "How

do you like that short — that sort o' shootin', mister?"

He grinned and it was contagious enough to make the stranger grin too, in understanding. There was a hint of arrogancy about this blond youngster and a touch of the flamboyant in his checkerboard shirt, fancy chaps and colored neckerchief, but there was nothing malicious in his spirit, the stranger decided. Blondie had absorbed enough liquor to see the repressions of sobriety as clay idols to be gaily shattered. That was all. With a shrug that dismissed the matter, the stranger crossed to the bar.

"Don't you go minding the younker, mister," the barkeep advised, low-voiced. "You'll get a new J. B. tomorrow. Likewise this damage he did will be settled for."

A wave of one pudgy hand took in a shattered bar mirror and a row of broken whiskey bottles. The stranger, eyeing the havoc, chuckled, guessing then why the lamps were unlighted although it was dark. To light a lamp would be to invite that target-hungry hell-raiser to shoot it out.

"He shore crowds his fun, don't he?" the stranger observed good-naturedly. "But likely the law will pick him up pronto if he isn't careful."

"The law? Dobe Kennedy won't take no

hand in this!" the barkeep snorted. "The marshal knows the Stormes have got their own law and he likewise knows yonder younker is 'going out' tonight. It'll be Storme law, not Battleweed law, that'll punish Tom Storme for his cavortin'."

"Tom Storme!" the stranger echoed, and the name had its significance, for he swung around for a second look. But big Tom Storme, his back to the bar, was at the gaming tables, boisterously handing out advice to a group of players.

"Yeah, that's Tom," the garrulous barkeep continued. "Don't reckon you ever seen him before, though, mister. You're looking at the youngest of the queerest tribe west o' the river. He's a grandson of old Joshua Storme, him they call 'Thunder'!"

The stranger nodded. "I've heard tell of Thunder Storme," he said, tight-lipped.

"Likely. The Stormes come here before my time — before any white man's time. Come from Texas, they say, with Thunder's herd and Thunder's crew. His wife was in a wagon with him, and his sons, Nahum and Noah and Nathan, just buttons then. There was a girl too, a baby, I've heard tell. Must 'a' been something like the Israelites lookin' for the Promised Land, that outfit, blazin' its way into this wilderness. They settled in the far end of Rearing Horse, running their cattle in the valley. Built a regular castle, with the cliffs to back it and a wall in front to keep folks out, just like them feudal lords you read about."

"That so?" the stranger said, but it was all the encouragement the barkeep needed.

"Keep-to-themselves sort o' folks," he explained. "It was forty-odd years ago they come. Thunder's sons is growed up now and have sons of their own now, like Tom there. And they all live at Storme Castle and Thunder sits on a regular throne and rules 'em, they say. Got their own laws and court and jail-house, so help me! Now take Tom there. Come tomorrow, Nahum Storme, his pappy, will be down here to pay for this damage. When Tom comes home his folks'll give him a trial for this hell-raisin'. Maybe he'll set in their hoosegow for thirty days over this little spree. He —"

Tom Storme had taken the stage again. In the middle of the floor once more, he flourished his gun, planted a bullet in the ceiling. *"Yee-ow!"* he shouted. "I'm the old man of the mountains and I ain't gettin' no younger! I'm a curly wolf and I'm howlin' till the moon howls back and then I'm gonna jump up there and bite a chunk outta it. I'm goin' out, gents, and I ain't aimin'

13

that Battleweed should forget me!"

The barkeep winked. "Reckon that 'goin' out' business has got you puzzled, stranger. When a Storme comes of age, they turn him loose to leave the valley for the first time and wander around a spell, wherever his trail takes him. Maybe he's gone a year, maybe five, but by and by he picks hisself a wife. Then he brings the missus back to Rearing Horse and settles down with the clan again. Tom's on his way out tonight, though some say he won't leave Battleweed. He's had his cap set for Sheila Merritt, old Doc Merritt's daughter."

Tom Storme was helping himself to a table bottle. "I'm the ridin'est rannyhan north o' the Rio," he announced loudly. "I hail from the Slashed S where hosses was invented. I can ride anything with a leg under it and a belly to cinch a saddle on."

"He hates himself plumb down to the ground," the stranger observed icily. "You figger there might be somebody in the whole damn world that could hogtie him?"

"Ain't been but one man that was ever big enough to defy the Stormes," the barkeep said gravely. "Dawson Reardon, he was. A right nice gent, as I remember him, a fellow about your build, stranger. He used to ride for the Stormes, about thirty years back —

14

which was when I first come here. But this Daw Reardon, he didn't hone to be anybody's hired man. He ups and marries and gets a ranch for himself down at this end o' the valley. By and by more small ranchers flocked in and the town of Battleweed started and begin growin'.

"Reckon that didn't suit old Thunder so well, him bein' lord of the whole shebang so long. One thing led to another, with talk of Storme cattle sprouting wings in the dark o' the moon. Finally there was out-and-out range war, the Slashed S ag'in the little fellers, with Daw Reardon leadin' the small ranchers. When Thunder hit, he hit hard! In one night he drove the small ranchers out of the valley. Daw Reardon was killed that night. His missus was already dead, died with childbirth, and young Stevie Reardon was took away by the other small ranchers, I reckon."

The stranger nodded slowly, lost in thought.

"That's the size of it," the barkeep concluded. "Fifteen years ago it was. Now there's small ranchers in the valley again, moved in these last five years. Some say trouble's shapin' all over again, but I'm wonderin'. The Stormes ruled Rearing Horse from the first. I reckon they'll rule it so long as there's a Storme still standing and able to trigger a gun. They cou—"

The barkeep broke a word in its middle as though it had just occurred to him that the stranger was no longer listening. Perhaps the barkeep also sensed the change that had come over the stranger. Perhaps he understood that his own words had been like some swift-working chemical that had wrought a transformation before his very eyes, changing the boy who'd come into the Buckhorn, carefree and tolerant, into a man with a purpose that manifested itself in a tightening of the stranger's rocky jaw.

"Get a grizzly bear up to the snubbing post!" Tom Storme was orating again. "Tighten the cinches on a catamount! I'll ride the critters! Me, I can —"

"Can you fight?" the stranger asked suddenly, and it was the way he said it that was both an insult and a challenge. "Can you use those big fists of yours — or do you just shoot off your gun and your face?"

Then there was thunderous silence, broken only by the scrape of chairs. The stranger hadn't spoken loudly. He scarcely raised his voice, yet he'd brought every eye upon him. Tom Storme stared, patently amazed and bewildered.

"I — I got no quarrel with you, stranger,"

he said. "What you makin' war-talk for?"

The stranger strode toward him, his boots making no noise on the sawdust strewn floor. "Maybe I've got a quarrel with you," he said as he faced the big youngster, and his hand moved. It was an open palm blow, a stinging slap that left fish-belly-hued fingermarks on Tom Storme's ruddy cheek. "Now, damn you," the stranger snapped, "will you fight?"

Tom Storme answered with action. Roaring wrathfully, he launched a fist, a man-crushing blow aimed for the stranger's head, a blow that would have ended the fight at its beginning if it had landed. But the stranger wasn't there. Dancing backward, keeping out of the way of flailing fists as Tom Storme tried to follow up, he unbuckled his gunbelt as he went, sending belt and holster clattering into a corner. He gave Tom time to unload himself in like fashion and then he was upon the youngster.

A wave of fists beat Tom Storme backward. But Tom was big and built for violence, and if whiskey spoiled his timing, it gave him an added zest for the fight. Slugging savagely, he moved in, hard-driven fists pistoning, and in that moment the stranger knew he had the fight of his life on his hands. Dodging Tom's mallet-like fists, getting under that windmill guard whenever he could, he pinned his faith in footwork, side-stepping, lashing back all the while.

It was hammer and tongs, the two of them swapping blows like men berserk. The stranger drew first blood, opening a cut over Tom's eye. But the stranger left himself open to accomplish that coup, and Tom beat him to his knees. The stranger's ears were roaring and a dozen Tom Stormes faced him as he came to his feet again, clinched until he regained his breath and a measure of his strength. Then he was dancing away, dancing in again, hammering relentlessly.

It was the rapier battling the bludgeon. The clamor of it drew men from the street, men who had ignored the Buckhorn when Tom Storme had been providing excitement with his gun but who couldn't ignore the lure of man-to-man combat. With the fight carrying the battlers to the far end of the room, crashing and clattering among the tables, someone succeeded in lighting the overhead lamps. From the corner of his eye the stranger glimpsed new faces in a growing ring of spectators, heard, as from a distance, the shouts and encouragements of the crowd without knowing whom they were shouting for.

Panting, he felt his power ebbing, did the stranger, and was consoled because Tom Storme was panting as well, his broad chest rising and falling. Bobbing beneath a blow, the stranger's fist exploded against Storme's jaw, leveling him.

"Give him the boot!" someone shouted. "Give it to him, stranger, while you've got him down!"

The stranger heard and understood, remembering then that the barkeep had spoken of a new influx of little ranchers into Rearing Horse and the recurrence of old hates and an ancient fight. But Tom Storme hadn't used his boots when the stranger had been upon his knees. A hate was goading this newcomer, a hate that all Rearing Horse would shortly savvy. But a code, stronger than the hate, couldn't be denied. He let Tom Storme come to his feet unscathed, waited while Tom stood there reeling, waited until Tom struck again before he launched his own fists.

It might have gone on forever. It might have lasted until both of them were bleeding and senseless, unconscious on their feet, too weary to lift their fists. But Tom Storme had come to his feet too soon. He was still groggy from the blow that had felled him and the stranger knew that his moment had come, the moment he'd played for from the first. He hit Tom, hit him with all the ragged remnants of his strength behind the blow, and Tom stretched inert in the sawdust.

It was over. Sobbing for breath, the stranger reeled to the bar, clung to it for a long time, the crowd — silent and awed — watching him wordlessly. Then the stranger found his sombrero, picked up his belt, latched it about his middle and patted his gun into place. A stringy man was elbowing officiously through the crowd.

"What's the ruckus about?" he wanted to know.

Marshal Dobe Kennedy was slack-jawed and shifty-eyed, a natural-born fence-straddler and therefore a natural-born politician, a tall stringy man as colorless as his own drab garb, as lusterless as the unpolished star that adorned his mouse-colored vest. A dozen men made bedlam as they found voices simultaneously and tried to explain, but the stranger silenced them all with a gesture.

"Look hereabouts at that bar mirror and those busted bottles and you can see the size of it for yourself, Marshal," he pointed. "Storme was looking for trouble. He found it when I got sick of seein' him look so hard.

Reckon you'll be jailing him for disturbin' the peace."

"Storme? Why — a — Battleweed law ain't never had no bolt on the Stormes. I can't —"

"He's in Battleweed, isn't he?" the stranger persisted. "Considering the bottles he's busted and the hell he's raised, I figger he's got about thirty days in the hoosegow coming to him. Now lock him up."

Marshal Dobe Kennedy, plainly in a split stick, caressed his receding jaw dubiously. "Shucks now," he said uneasily, "I can't do that. The Stormes would come down here and tear the jail apart — and the town too, likely. I —"

The stranger sneered. "So they've got you buffaloed along with the rest, eh? They've got you so you can't even law your own town the way you should. Give me your keys then. I'll lock him up for you!"

Dobe Kennedy made a half-hearted attempt at belligerency. "Now just a minit —" he began.

"Give me your keys!" the stranger ordered, and something in his stormy eyes made Dobe Kennedy hastily lower his own gaze and paw into his pockets for a key ring which he extended.

Pocketing the keys, the stranger stooped,

grasped an arm of the unconscious Tom Storme. With an effort he got the big youngster over his shoulder, lurched erect. For a moment the saloon and the spectators spun about him and the sickening thought swept him that his knees were going to cave. He fought desperately against the nausea that threatened to engulf him, gritting his teeth and fastening his eyes upon the batwings which seemed miles away. And, fighting, he conquered the surging weakness.

Glancing neither to the left nor to the right, he stalked from that silence-stricken saloon, lurched up the street, thankful that the jail-building huddled not too far away, a squat toad in the gloom.

Behind him men suddenly found their tongues as though with his departure a spell had been lifted. The stranger couldn't hear them, but he smiled grimly in the friendly darkness, for he knew what they were saying. He'd seen a startled look in the barkeep's eyes when the lamps had been lighted. That barkeep had recognized him and with recognition the barkeep had understood why he'd forced a fight upon Tom Storme.

There'd be news in Battleweed this night, startling news, news that would spread as wildfire spreads before the prairie wind, until all of Rearing Horse heard it.

"Steve Reardon is back!" they'd be saying. "Dawson Reardon's kid has come home growed up. I tell you it's so! You can't mistake him — he's the spittin' image of Daw years ago. Looks like he's taking up his paw's old fight against the Stormes! He's buyin' a war for hisself, that's what he's doin'!"

And Steve Reardon, son of the only man who'd ever defied the Stormes, staggered along with Tom Storme upon his back, glorying in one soul-satisfying thought. They'd have to admit that he'd won the first battle!

two

This was the manner in which Steve Reardon returned to Rearing Horse Valley with his gun dedicated to vengeance, returned to take up a fight that had climaxed in gun-flame and bloodshed fifteen long years ago. Lone-handed he was challenging the might of the Storme clan and lone-handed he'd already tossed down the gauntlet. Yet his first victory gave him no false illusions, for this was only a beginning. Now he walked with death and the trail ahead was long and treacherous and uncertain.

But Steve was content to let the future take care of itself as he climbed the steps of the jail-building. The door opened into the marshal's office which faced onto the street, with a second door leading from the office into the cell corridor. Lugging Tom Storme into the building, Steve deposited the unconscious youngster upon the floor while he fumbled in the darkness to get a lamp aglow. With shadows mottling the littered desk, dancing across the fly-specked reward dodgers on the walls, he explored the cell row and, finding it empty, dragged Tom into a cell. Experimenting until he found the proper key, he locked its door.

Tom Storme had been battered into insensibility, but the fight had taken its toll of Steve, too, for he ached in every muscle. Tossing the key ring to the desk and blowing out the lamp, he left the building and went to the nearest horse-trough and washed his face. The water was cold enough, the shock of it serving to clear his head to some degree. He was mopping his face with his neckerchief when the stringy form of Dobe Kennedy loomed in the darkness.

"Jasper Galt wants to see you," the town marshal informed him surlily. "You'll find his office next door to the bank."

"And who is this fellow Galt," Steve demanded, "that a gent's supposed to jump just because he barks?"

"Galt is head man in Battleweed, seein' as how he just about owns the town. Some call him 'Spider' Galt, but not to his face. Was I you, I'd trot along."

Steve shrugged. He couldn't recall Spider Galt, but his memory of Battleweed and its people was sketchy in many respects. He didn't like being sent for as though he were some sort of servant, but he was curious to see what manner of man ordered others about and that curiosity bent his footsteps toward Galt's office.

He was halfway down the street, a thing of light and shadow now that lamps varnished a patch of yellow before each unwashed window and pools of darkness lay between, before it dawned upon him that a gaping rip had marked the spot on Dobe Kennedy's drab vest where the marshal's badge had been.

That was queer, Steve decided, and passed the Buckhorn where men now lined the bar. The place was doing a flourish business and the hum of excited voices, reaching Steve, made him grin, for he could guess the nature of the talk. Then he was on down the street, turning into Spider Galt's office. It was a cubby-hole of a place, musty and almost bare of furniture, and he forgot his speculation about Dobe Kennedy and the excitement in the Buckhorn as a man greeted him from behind a flat-topped desk. Overhead a dim, smoky lamp flickered, leaving the corners of this box-like room in shadows.

"Sit down, Stephen Reardon," the man invited.

This, then, was Spider Galt and, facing the fellow, Steve was able to reach into some shadowy recess of his memory and, doing

26

so, he knew he had seen the man before. Galt was a tall man, so tall that his lanky body was folded into a sort of inverted *N* to accommodate itself to his chair. He was a creature all arms and legs, a man bony of frame and bony of feature, an animated skeleton with arched Mephistophelian eyebrows and shrewd, unblinking eyes and dank, dark hair so thin as to make his high forehead seem even higher. The rusty black suit that garbed him made him none the less repellent and somehow Steve was glad Galt didn't proffer his hand.

"You know me?" Steve asked.

"News travels fast," Galt chuckled. "All Battleweed knows you by now, but I'd have recognized you anyway, I believe. I knew your father, Reardon — and your mother. You see, I've been here for a long time, since before the first building went up in Battleweed. And I've fought the Stormes for a long time, almost since that first day — fought them tooth and nail and earned their hatred. Now can you understand why I sent for you?"

A chair stood before the desk and Steve eased into it. "It begins to make savvy," he acknowledged.

Galt leaned forward, his bony fingers interlocking. "Tell me, why did you choose fists against Tom Storme tonight?" he asked. "Can't you use that gun you're wearing?"

"I'm fair to middlin' with it," Steve confessed. "In fact, I reckon I'd have killed him if I'd uncorked a smokepole. Which is exactly why I didn't. Tom's just come of age, which means he was six years old when Dawson Reardon was murdered. It follows that he certainly couldn't have been the one that pulled that trigger."

Galt elevated one eyebrow, "Hmmm," he mused. "Your feud, then, is only against the one Storme who killed your father. You hold no grudge against the others?"

Steve's dark eyes snapped. "I hate them all!" he said emphatically. "I aim to see them driven from Rearing Horse. I aim to match smoke with any of them that crave to test my iron — and I'm hopin' every last man of 'em will take a whack at it. But there's something else I've got to do to 'em first — hit 'em where it hurts the most. Pride! That's their long suit! So first I aim to drag 'em off their high horse, make 'em eat dirt. When a man's dead, he's that way for a long time, and nothing makes any difference to a dead man. Killin' the pack of 'em wouldn't half satisfy me!"

He paused and his voice grew more

28

brittle. "That's why I licked Tom, tossed him in jail tonight instead of killing him. That's my first slap at Thunder Storme's face! At showdown I'll get the one that killed my dad. And the gunsmoke will smell sweeter if I can make the others point him out to save their own yellow souls! But say! Maybe you know which one beefed Daw?"

Galt shrugged. "It's hard to say. I was with the small ranchers that night, but I wasn't with your father when he fell. It was the Ox who picked him up. I guess the big galoot couldn't tell a Storme from an enemy."

"The Ox?"

"The half-wit. The giant that's worked for the Stormes ever since anybody can remember. Came from Texas with them, I guess. But maybe you wouldn't remember him from the old days."

Steve shook his head. The Ox . . . ? There was something tantalizingly familiar about the odd name and the fragmentary description, but he couldn't conjure anything concrete from his memory — not then.

Jasper Galt smiled. "You and I," he said, "will get along, I think. Supposing I told you that your fight was my fight? Supposing I told you I hated the Stormes as much as you do? What would you say if I suggested we tie together in this thing?"

"Just what's your stake?" Steve asked bluntly.

"I helped build Battleweed to what it is," Galt said. "It's my town. I want to see it flourish and go ahead — and I want all of Rearing Horse to build for better days. The Stormes want to keep it part of the past. There's some talk that Dakota and Western intend to lay steel this way. If the railroad comes through here one of these days, it will bring prosperity to all of us. Do you think the Stormes would allow the D & W right of way through the valley? Not a chance! If progress is to come, the Stormes have got to go."

"And you figger that you and me can drive them out, eh?"

"The two of us — and the others who want the right to live here," Galt amended. "History is due to repeat itself, Reardon. Small ranchers have come in again and the Stormes don't like it and the same old trouble is shaping up. But perhaps the outcome will be different this time."

"Sounded like there was some folks down at the saloon when me and Tom was tossin' fists that wasn't exactly in love with the clan," Steve observed, remembering those who had urged him to use his boots on the fallen youngster.

"The Stormes are growing soft, decadent, from too many years of ruling the roost," Galt went on. "Old Thunder hasn't shown his face out of the castle for years and his sons are scarcely ever in Battleweed except at the time of the annual rodeo, which comes off at the end of this week. Why, they don't even do their own fighting any more! They've brought in Anse Tarn and those thirty-odd professional gun-slingers of his — the pack folks call the Sixty Six-Guns."

Steve started. "The Sixty Six-Guns! I know all about that bunch! The big ranchers along Milk River hired them to drive out the sodbusters not long ago. You mean to say that crew is working for the Stormes?"

Again Galt shrugged. "When a small rancher finds his barn burned or his fences cut, the Sixty Six-Guns are usually in the offing. Who else could they be working for in this valley? They're a hardcase crew, but maybe we'll be able to match them. I was a friend of your dad and the small ranchers before. I'm organizing the little fellers again, lending them money to build with and to buy bullets. But I need a fighting man to do the leading. And now I think I've found the man."

He dipped a bony hand into a desk drawer

and the badge that had adorned Dobe Kennedy's vest winked in the lamplight.

"This is yours, if you want it. It will give you the law's authority in Battleweed and the small ranchers will respect it. You'll have the legal authority to back up the play you made tonight, to keep Tom Storme in jail if you choose. Kennedy was a good enough marshal so long as nobody cracked a cap, but he proved tonight what I've long suspected — that he wouldn't buck the Stormes if it came to a showdown. You will."

Steve fingered the badge: "Isn't there some kind of procedure when a marshal is ousted and a new one appointed to finish the term?" he asked dubiously. "Doesn't some kind of committee have the say? Don't seem right —"

"*I'll* worry about that," Spider Galt chuckled. "This is *my* town, Reardon. When you pin on that badge, you're the law in Battleweed."

Steve Reardon hesitated, but that was because he needed time for thinking. He'd learned much in this talk with Spider Galt. He'd learned that the odds against him were even greater than he'd anticipated, for the dread Sixty Six-Guns, specialists in terrorism, had to be reckoned with. He knew that outfit and its reputation — an unsavory crew who hired their guns to the highest bidder and didn't hesitate to put bullets between shoulder blades if necessary.

But Steve had also learned there was a faction that might side him, the small ranchers — and Spider Galt was leader of that faction. But that was the very reason for Steve's hesitancy. He didn't like Spider Galt, sensing instinctively that the man dealt cards from either end of the deck when the occasion demanded. That same instinct told him Spider Galt had no real love for him, either. Yet Steve polished the badge against his sleeve and pinned it on.

Galt smiled, shuffled papers on his desk, a gesture that Steve took as a signal of dismissal. "Drop in again, Marshal," Galt said. "How long do you intend to keep Tom Storme in *your* jail?"

Steve grinned. "About thirty days, I reckon. Maybe some of his relatives might come and visit him."

He stepped into the night, but with darkness around him, he gave himself to reflection as he strode away. Things were moving fast and once again he'd scored a victory, but he couldn't shake away the feeling that he'd made himself Spider Galt's man when he'd accepted the badge. It wasn't to Steve's liking to be another Dobe Kennedy who couldn't call his soul his own.

Still, he'd gained an important ally and the proof of it was on every hand. Here was the bank building, a stone structure swathed in darkness, bearing the name of Jasper Galt in gold letters across its broad window. Next door was the land office legended in like fashion. By Dobe Kennedy's say-so and Galt's own admission, this was Galt's town. Steve Reardon and Jasper Galt were partners in a common cause. And truly Jasper Galt would be a better friend than an enemy for the proof was here that Galt was a power in Battleweed.

But no human power can stop a bullet. And Steve, wrapped in his conflicting thoughts, had no inkling that death stalked him on this dark street. He was only remotely aware that he'd come abreast of a slot between two buildings, a void peopled with shadows. Then, suddenly, those shadows blossomed with gun-flame — once, twice . . .

For the second time in the brief period since he'd ridden into Battleweed, Steve felt the airlash of a bullet, saw his sombrero go sailing. But whoever was triggering now wasn't shooting as Tom Storme had shot —

for the fun of seeing a man jump. This gunman was playing for keeps. There was proof enough of that as the second bullet creased Steve's shoulder, turning it into a thing of fire and agony.

three

Flinging himself to the ground, Steve clawed for his gun as he dropped, but even in that perilous moment he found time to reflect that already the Stormes knew of his presence here, for there was no one else in all of Rearing Horse who might have reason to murder him. After that, all thought gave way to action as he thumbed shots into the darkness, shooting in the direction of those gunflashes, spreading bullets wide and at random in the hope that he might score a hit.

Rolling as he fired, Steve made a mighty poor target and the darkness that screened the killer screened Steve as well. But that same factor made shooting haphazard — a deadly game of blind man's buff with bullets to do the tagging. One geysered dust near Steve's face, another nicked a boot heel while lead hummed waspishly past his ear. Those bullets were close — mighty close! With an angry oath, Steve came to his feet. He might have retreated into the darkness, but he wasn't in a mood for discretion, so instead he lunged between the buildings to carry the fight to the enemy.

Thudding boot heels told him the other was fleeing, but the proof of it only goaded Steve anew. It was blacker than the inside of a steer's stomach back here and Steve tripped, stumbled over heaped debris. Picking himself up, he paused, panting, his ears cocked, his eyes strained.

For one fleeting moment Steve saw a tall, stringy form dart across a patch of light streaming from a rear window farther down the alley. That brief glimpse was all he had and then the killer was gone.

Dobe Kennedy? That unknown had seemed to be about Kennedy's build, but it was hard to be sure, for the glimpse hadn't lasted the length of a wink. Had Kennedy resented his replacement as marshal and chosen this method of retaliation? An undercover killing would be in keeping with the man's obvious spinelessness.

Yet Steve, reasoning the thing out, didn't believe his own deductions. His first anger had died, and with reason reasserting itself, he knew that it was both senseless and dangerous to seek the man in this murk. Giving up the fruitless chase, he groped his way back to the street where he found a knot of excited, questioning men gathering.

Steve dusted his sombrero, eyed the second bullet hole speculatively. "The fun's all over, gents," he told them. "Guess maybe the Stormes have already heard that one of their kinfolk is in jail. They just tried to bail him out, but they were putting up lead instead of silver. Where'll I find a sawbones?"

His shoulder pained him and his shirt was soggy with blood. Someone pointed up the street. "Doc Merritt lives yonder, almost at the edge of town. Watch for his nameplate and you can't miss the place."

Steve nodded and headed in the indicated direction. Now the moon was aloft and the silver mist, filtering through the tree tops, made a lacy pattern across the ground. Striding along, he came at last to a white cottage, vine-covered and flower-fringed. Light glowed in its windows and a wisp of smoke eddied from the chimney and the whole of it was like something from a picture book.

For a long moment Steve paused there, chained by something nameless that stirred within him, and his eyes were hungry and in them was the sort of loneliness that is embodied in the coyote's howl or the whisper of wind in high mountain passes. The picket fence gate bore the nameplate of Dr. Joseph Merritt. Fumbling with the latch, Steve admitted himself, walked up a flagstone path to the porch and raised an ancient iron knocker.

The girl who opened the door wore a white dress and, framed in the doorway, she was like a white flame. Tall and supple, she was firm-breasted in the full-bodied bloom of womanhood, a sweet-faced thing with blue-black hair, the color of Steve's own, cascading to her shoulders. All these things Steve saw at a glance, but there was more that he sensed — the virginity of her that might have been symbolized by her dress, the depth of her character that lay in the depth of her eyes. Instinctively he cradled his sombrero against his chest.

"I'm lookin' for Doc Merritt, miss," he said.

Her eyes were blue and her smile warmed them. "Steve!" she exclaimed. "Steve Reardon! Oh, we heard you were back! Don't you remember me — Sheila Merritt?"

His face must have betrayed his bewilderment. The name meant nothing to him, only that it served to remind him of something the garrulous barkeep at the Buckhorn had said and the words came back to him now. "Tom's on his way out tonight, though some say he won't leave Battleweed," the fellow had explained. "He's had his cap set for Sheila Merritt, old

Doc Merritt's daughter."

This, then, was Doc Merritt's daughter and he, Steve, was supposed to remember her, but he didn't. She pretended to pout.

"Have you forgotten the valley school and the girl with the long pigtails that you used to tease so unmercifully? I'm disappointed, Steve. You see, I remembered the boy who was the leader of the other little boys, just as his father was leader of the ranchers. But come in, Steve. Dad is home."

She ushered him into a lamp-lighted living room, furnished for comfort, but his glance scarcely touched the scattered chairs, the centering book-littered table, the fireplace that was cheerful without a fire, for he was fumbling for words. "I — I do remember now. You've changed some, miss. I —"

But Doc Merritt was here to rescue him — Doc Merritt, tall and silver-maned, kindly of face and stooped of figure, his shoulders beneath his black coat rounded from carrying the weight of a range's woes for two score years. He came from the depth of a chair, his cherubic face beaming, his hand outstretched. And the years rolled back for Steve Reardon, for he recalled this man from yesterday, and with the recollection he also remembered the measles and every other disease that was created, seemingly, for the sole purpose of bedeviling little boys.

"Welcome home, boy! Welcome home," Doc said. "The whole town is afire with talk of you. I've been hoping you'd call on us. Man, but you look like Daw Reardon! But you're wounded!"

"A scratch," Steve said. "It was the Stormes' way of welcoming me home. Somebody shot at me from cover not fifteen minutes ago."

Doc Merritt was already reaching for his black case perched atop the mantelpiece, and Sheila, trained by a lifetime of such emergencies, darted for the kitchen to fetch hot water and towels, her heels beating a rhythmic tattoo against the floor. Doc fumbled with his bag.

"The Stormes?" he asked. "Are you sure, son? It was never their way to shoot from cover, even though they might not be eager to have you with us again. You see, I know why you're back, boy. All Battleweed knows it, or has guessed it. But an attempt at murder — Could it be that your hate has blinded you?"

"Hate?" Steve echoed as Doc Merritt began to cut his shirt away. "Don't you think I'm entitled to hate? You were here in the old days. You know the reasons I have to hate them."

"Aye, I was here. Your father died in my arms."

Steve lifted his eyes with new interest. "He did! Did he talk? Tell me, did he know which one of them got him? Did he tell you?"

Sheila came with the water and Doc methodically swabbed the wound before replying. The bullet had plowed a bloody furrow before winging on its way, but it had done little more than break the skin.

"Dawson Reardon was shot in the back," Doc Merritt explained. "That is why, to this day, I don't believe the Stormes got him, unless they did so accidentally. There was a lot of lead tossed that night. As the Stormes swept down the valley, the little ranchers retreated before them, one by one, fighting every inch of the way, and the bunch of them made a last stand at your dad's Rolling R. The Stormes ringed them there and it was hell among the daisies. Shucks, in the darkness and all, one of your dad's own friends might have got him by mistake."

"That would make it simple," Steve said bitterly, and winced involuntarily as iodine stung him. "That would wipe the slate clean, wouldn't it? All except for the little

42

fact that the Stormes came with guns to drive free men from free land, just so they could hog Rearing Horse Valley, keep it for themselves!"

Doc Merritt sought shelter in silence. Working away, he soon had pad and ties in place and a bandage over it all. Steve wormed into the torn remnants of his shirt.

"Talk," Doc Merritt reflected thoughtfully, "comes cheaper than a heap of things. I learned that simple truth years back, but still I talk too much. I see you're wearing a badge, Steve. Only one man in Battleweed could have given it to you. I might say things that would make you think twice about lining up with Spider Galt — but I won't. That's your business. But tell me, boy, is there no swerving you? Must you stay and fight?"

"Yes," said Steve, and knew that Sheila's eyes were upon him, heavy with thought. "I must."

Doc Merritt shrugged, looking more stooped than ever as though his years had gathered weight in these last few minutes.

"Stephen," he said, "whether you know it or not, I brought you into this world. And I worked without sleep for seventy-two hours trying to pull your mother through afterwards. I called Dawson Reardon my friend

43

— and saw him die. Those things were part of my job. But because I did those things, will you listen to an old man who has lived a lot longer than you have? Will you take my advice and forget this feud and ride away?"

Steve, hearing the ring of sincerity in that tired, old voice, averted his eyes. "I'm thankin' you, Doc," he said. "Believe me, I wish I could see it your way. But you say you called Daw Reardon friend — and saw him die. It's the last I can't forget. I'm sorry, Doc — but the answer is still no."

Again Doc Merritt was silent, the minutes lock-stepping by. "I've been here a long time," he said at last. "I've seen bloodshed and smelled gunsmoke and taken no sides. It's for others to maim and to kill — it's for me to heal and to save. That's my stand and it will be my stand when trouble comes again — as come it will, just as surely as darkness follows daylight.

"Nearly forty years ago I first crossed palms with Thunder Storme, a strange man, a fighter who was at the same time a lover of peace. He left Texas because he hated the strife during and after the war between the states. He loaded his family into a wagon and he drove his herd before him and he headed north by west seeking one thing — a place where he could order his life and

44

the life of his loved ones as he saw fit. Can you believe that, Steve?

"And perhaps he'd have preferred peace when he waged war on your father and his friends. Who knows? There are things that only time and God can answer. But there is something else, son, something I'd like to tell you but can't. As a doctor, I'm the only outsider who has ever been admitted into Storme Castle. I know things that others don't even suspect — secrets that were entrusted to me in my professional capacity. And I know that if you pursue this feud, you will live to regret it.

"Perhaps you'll lose, which will mean six feet of earth beside your father — providing that someone is considerate enough to plant you there. Perhaps you'll win — and know the truth for yourself. For if I have judged you right — if I know you as I think I know you — then I say that the day you stand before Thunder's throne will be the sorriest day of your life!"

It was a long speech and Steve gave it due consideration, standing gravely and in silence, the eyes of the father and daughter upon him. He adjusted his sombrero carefully and just as carefully laid a gold piece upon the table. He took a step toward the door before he spoke.

"There is much to think about in what you have said," he agreed. "But you are speaking from your own heart and you are a tolerant man. I might have learned tolerance, too — if I'd had a father when a boy needs a father, if I'd had a share of kindness and consideration and the things that breed tolerance. But don't you see? *They* robbed me of that. As it is — the answer's the same. Good night, sir."

Doc Merritt stepped aside, beaten. But Sheila came to Steve now, laid a hand upon his arm, her eyes liquid as she lifted them to meet his own solemn stare.

"You hurt a woman's pride tonight, Steve," she said. "You'd forgotten me completely when I'd remembered you — all these long years. Perhaps you owe me something for that. Then believe me when I say that Dad is right. Go, Steve, and forget your hate."

In that moment she was so utterly appealing that the words to deny her wouldn't come. Yet Steve had to remember that Tom Storme's name had been linked with hers, that it was common knowledge in Battleweed that Tom Storme would look no farther than this cottage for the wife he was supposed to seek.

Was there an understanding between the

two of them? Was it for Tom's sake that she wanted him, Steve, to leave? Steve didn't know, but the thought left him with a queer sense of emptiness that both puzzled and alarmed him. He framed words to answer her, but he never spoke them.

Down the street guns barked, staccato and strident, making bedlam of the night, jerking the three of them as though they were so many puppets attached to strings. Intermingled with that deadly thunder were the hoarse shouts of men, the drumbeat of racing hoofs. Instantly Sheila was to the window, thrusting the curtains apart, hoisting the shade and the sash. She leaned outside and then turned back to them, her face chalky.

"It's the Sixty Six-Guns!" she exclaimed. "I could see them. They've ridden into town! They're surrounding the jail!"

The Sixty Six-Guns! The hired gun-hands who did the bidding of the Storme clan!

Doc Merritt tottered toward the window. "Put out the light!" he ordered. "When that pack starts throwing lead, they're not particular who it might hit. Sheila, get on the floor! Steve — !"

But Steve Reardon, sensing just why the guncrew was storming the jail and knowing that the victory he'd gained this night would be lost if the wolf pack succeeded in delivering Tom Storme from the jail, was already darting through the doorway.

four

Chaos was king in Battleweed, the street a milling maelstrom of scurrying men, for Anse Tarn and his Sixty Six-Guns had come and the citizenry was making a general rush for cover, with bullets speeding them on their way. With a leader to rally them, those townspeople might have made a concerted stand — but there was no leader. All that Steve saw and sensed as he paused on the porch of the Merritt cottage. Then he was running — sprinting desperately down the street to where those horsemen massed before the jail.

They'd struck so suddenly, those raiders, as to catch Steve completely unprepared. He'd expected the Stormes might use their hired gunhands to snatch Tom from the jail, but hadn't expected they'd make such a move so soon. The fact that they had, only made Steve more determined to spoil this plan of theirs somehow. His gun in his hand, Steve stampeded forward and, triggering, he charged among the horsemen, carrying the fight to them. For with doors banging open and the street awash with light, the raiders had already marked him and lead was zipping his way.

"It's the new badge-toter!" a gunhog shouted. "Burn the fist-slingin' son down!"

Somebody with an ear for an alliteration had dubbed this pack the Sixty Six-Guns. Whether there were actually thirty of them was hard to guess, impossible at this moment, and probably only a fraction of the bunch were two-gun men. But all of them were adept at assassination, and if they hadn't been packed too closely for effective shooting, Steve would have died before that first leaden hail.

Dodging and dancing, shifting from shadow to shadow, making himself as elusive a target as possible, Steve unleashed his lead. He was right among them, and a horseman loomed gargantuan in his nearness. Steve had one brief glimpse of a flat, stolid face and eyes white-hot with killer-lust. He saw bearded lips writhing in a grimace of savage satisfaction as the man tilted his gun.

He was almost upon Steve, this man who made a business of murder, his horse rearing. Steve shot him between the eyes with no more compunction than if he were shooting a ravening wolf — shot him just as the fellow tightened his finger on the trigger of his own gun. The bullet sent dust spurting as the gunhog sagged.

With the man somersaulting from the saddle, Steve was snatching frantically at the reins, vaulting into the hull he'd just emptied. He was mounted now, a dubious advantage, for only luck was keeping him alive and that luck couldn't last against such odds. Strategy might save him, but there wasn't time to plan strategy.

Instinctively Steve wheeled his horse against the nearest gunman's and by that action he spoiled the fellow's aim. A gun blazed, almost in Steve's face. Kicking his feet free of the stirrups as the two horses collided, Steve hurled himself upon the man.

Once, in a little town along Milk River where the Sixty Six-Guns had come to hire out for devil's work, Steve, passing through, had gotten a look at their leader, Anse Tarn. Now, as he wrapped his arms around his adversary, he was only aware that he was gripping a big red-faced, thick-necked gorilla of a man. They'd thudded to the ground together, a twisting, sprawling knot of arms and legs, before Steve realized he was grappling with Tarn himself, kingpin of this viper's brood. Here was more luck, incentive enough to give Steve new strength.

They were down in the dust with horses

rearing and plunging all around them, lashing hoofs leaving a grim reminder that both of them might be brained in a matter of minutes. Sweat blinded Steve, but he managed to twist Tarn's right arm behind the fellow's back and jerk upward.

Steve's bandage was slipping and he could feel blood worming down his side, hot and sticky. But he succeeded in forcing Tarn to his feet and he poked a gun-barrel into Tarn's ribs with his free hand.

To a chorus of startled curses, the Sixty Six-Guns were spreading out. Disconcerted by the unhorsing of their leader, holding their fire for fear they might shoot Tarn while trying to kill Steve, they had been helpless momentarily. Now they were fanning wide for effective shooting. Steve, his voice desperate, shouted above the thudding hoofs.

"Steady on those triggers!" he cried. "Steady! Crack another cap and I'll put a slug plumb through this skunk!"

Then he was dragging Tarn toward the jail-building for Steve's back was exposed and in that factor lay the weakness of this grim gamble born of desperation. The Sixty Six-Guns were temporarily paralyzed, amazed by this swift turn of events. Yet this was one of those hell-freighted moments when time seemed to stand still, for the spell Steve had cast was a fragile thing and nobody knew it better than himself.

But he backed to the building unscathed and by that very act he accomplished his coup, for on the jail steps he held the cursing Tarn before him, a human shield.

"Vamoose!" Steve shouted. "I'm givin' you hombres just sixty seconds to get to hell out of town, or I'll blow this galoot in two!"

Silence suddenly spread over Battleweed like a heavy shroud, a thunderous silence in which the jingle of a bit chain, the creak of a restless saddle were explosive things, magnified all out of proportion. There was hesitancy and hatred in the faces of that semicircle of riders who were the Sixty Six-Guns. Someone, reaching a decision, mouthed a vile imprecation and gestured toward a gun.

It was like one of those times when a man stakes everything on a turn of roulette and the wheel hesitates between red and black and takes an eternity before stopping. But suddenly Anse Tarn was finding his voice.

"Do as he says!" he shrieked. "I ain't hankerin' for lead in my guts!"

Steve had counted on just such a reaction as this, pinned his faith in it from the first. These were killers, hunting in a pack, but

Steve had guessed that any one of them, individually, was yellow to the core — including their leader. Tarn, his face livid, cursed in a babbling voice, and Steve grinned inwardly, sensing a certain irony here, for this man was begging his own followers not to endanger his life. Someone wheeled a horse. Another followed suit — and another and another. Then dust was boiling and the Sixty Six-Guns were vanishing into the night, vanishing just as quickly as they'd appeared. Steve found himself alone with their leader.

Battleweed's street was only deserted for a minute and then men began to appear, edging into view from doorways and the slots between buildings. Steve chose the moment to make his last play.

He might have dragged Anse Tarn to a cell. He decided against it, his mind working swiftly. The Sixty Six-Guns had made this abortive attempt to rescue Tom Storme. They might think twice before trying that again. But if Tarn were jailed they'd have no choice but to rescue him in order to save their reputation. Steve didn't want to have to camp continually on the jail steps from now on.

Plucking Tarn's gun from its holster, Steve hurled the weapon into the darkness.

Then he booted Tarn down the steps, sending the man sprawling face forward into the dust. "Get your tail between your legs and follow your pack!" Steve ordered scathingly. "Pronto, feller! The smell of you stinks up this town!"

Anse Tarn picked himself up, his broad face aflame, his blocky body quivering. He was sobbing with wrath and impotence as he shook a beefy fist at Steve, his anger so great that it made him thick of tongue. "You win this time, star-toter!" he snarled. "You've taken this hand, but the game's just started. There'll be another time, savvy — *my time!* I'm darin' yuh to set foot in the upper valley just once! I'll see yuh staked out on an ant-hill! I'll —"

The rest of it was blistering invective that seared the air. It lasted until Tarn pulled himself into a saddle, hurtled after his crew. Steve had stood watching him coldly, a humorless smile upon his lips, a smile that had only infuriated Tarn the more. Now Steve heaved an explosive sigh. The men of Battleweed were edging forward, congratulations upon their lips. Steve put his back to them.

Stalking into the jail-building, he had a look at Tom Storme. The big blond youngster was conscious now, seated on the edge of the cot that furnished the cell, his head in his hands. He didn't look up while Steve stood there, so Steve returned to the office, closing the door to the cell corridor after him, and got the desk lamp aglow. He sagged into a chair, the aftermath of the excitement sawing at his nerves. He was adjusting his bandage when he heard the creak of the outer door and the scrape of sole-leather and raised his eyes to find Sheila in the room.

"Steve," she said, her eyes shining. "I saw it all from our porch. It was magnificent!"

A shawl, draped across her shoulders, made her no less appealing than she'd been at the cottage. Steve gulped. "But Tarn's outfit works for the Stormes," he blurted. "From the way you folks talked, I sorta figgered you and your dad favored the Stormes."

"The small ranchers are convinced that the Sixty Six-Guns were hired by the Stormes to bedevil them. But Dad and I don't believe it."

He smiled skeptically. "You came here to tell me that?"

"No. I came because I asked a favor of you up home. I asked you to forget your feud for my sake — if not for Dad's or your own. You didn't have a chance to answer me before you ran out."

Steve came to his feet and found a chair for her. He eyed her in silence for a long moment after she was seated, grave with the realization that somehow he must make her understand his feelings in the matter.

"I'll give you your answer — by spinnin' a yarn for you," he decided at last. ". . . A story that starts here in the valley where I was born. Care to listen?"

She nodded and it was encouragement enough.

"I can't remember much about those first years," he confessed. "Now that I'm seeing familiar sights and faces, things are beginning to come back to me, but a lot of it is still pretty dim. After I saw your dad again, I remembered him, and you — a little gal, mostly eyes. And I remember the Stormes — big, blond fellers like Tom, riding the valley like they was lords of creation. And — and I remember a night with guns spitting and horses squealing — the night that my dad died . . ."

"I know," she murmured. "Tell me, Steve, what became of you that night? Dad always supposed that some of the evicted small ranchers took you along with them when they fled from the valley."

"When the Stormes closed in on us and it

looked like the finish, Dad made me scoot into the darkness," he explained. "I got away, crawling on my stomach, dodging from one shadow to another, but a stray bullet clipped my head. I remember fainting and I remember coming to all alone. There was a big moon and the night was so still you could hear the hush. I walked for miles. I was plenty thirsty and my head ached and — and I cried a little. And then is where the queer part comes . . .

"It seems like a lady picked me up, a lady in a buckboard. I wish I could be sure. Yet I've got a recollection of followin' a road of sorts, stumblin' along, and her coming and bandaging my head and loading me onto the seat. Seems like we rode for hours, never saying a word to each other. Finally we stopped at a crossroads, just before dawn, and she flagged a stage that come along. She loaded me onto the stage and gave the driver an envelope. There was money in it — I heard it clink."

Sheila's eyes widened. "This lady? What did she look like?"

"Like a queen," Steve said reverently. "She was tall and sorta dignified and her face was proud and pretty at the same time. Like the picture of a grand lady I saw in a museum in Chicago one time when I went back there with a trainload of beef. She was gray-haired but she didn't look so old. And yet, dang it, sometimes I believe I just dreamed the whole thing. Sometimes I'm sure I was out of my head with fever and that part of it never really happened."

Lost in thought, Sheila drummed her fingertips on the desk top. "Perhaps it never did," she decided. "Or perhaps your ghost lady was the wife of one of the small ranchers who recognized you when she found you and took steps to see that you got clear of the valley."

Steve shrugged. "Next thing I remember is being at a ranch run by an old couple, name of Dillon. The stage driver must have left me there. Now I know that the ranch was up in the Flathead country, but at the time it was just mountain country to me, enough like the Bitter Root to make me feel at home. I don't remember much about it. I missed my dad a heap, but the old folks were mighty kind to me. They died two years later, when I was eleven, so I never did get around to asking them about my 'ghost lady,' which I'd have probably done if they'd lived till I was older."

"And then — ?"

Steve's jaw tightened. "Then I was homeless. The Dillons owed a heap of money and the sheriff took the ranch and put it up for auction. I drifted that same day. After that I saw the Powder River and I saw the Rio — and below it. Mostly I swamped in saloons for a bed and grub — with kicks and cuffs thrown in. Those were hard years, Sheila, years I'd rather forget. Those were the years when I saw other youngsters with time to play — and folks to love 'em.

"Sometimes I'd prowl around a town at night and I'd see those little cottages like you and your dad have got up the street. I'd peek in the windows and there'd be folks sittin' at supper tables with the kids coaxing an extra slab of pie outa the old folks. I'd stand there lookin', seein' the love they had for each other, and something would get tight inside me and I couldn't stand to watch. And that's when I began to hate the Stormes. Can you savvy? They took my dad. A gun can even that score. But they also took my boyhood away from me, took the things I might have had — and nothing can settle for that!"

She could only nod, her eyes averted.

"I got ridin' jobs when I was a little older," Steve went on. "And that's when I first got my big idea. At one of the spreads where I worked, the ramrod had a son, a kid who aimed to be a doctor. Every time that button got a chance to work on something that needed healing, he was on the job. He was preparing himself, savvy, for the job he was going to do later on. That's when I figgered out that I had a job to do likewise and the trick was to prepare myself for it. I had to get ready to come back and settle with the Stormes.

"They were big, I knew. Licking them was going to be a man-sized job. I got books and schooled myself, reading in bunkhouses and line-camps and taking a heap of hoorawin' from my pards. But mostly I schooled myself with a gun. I pestered every gunhand I met, got 'em to teach me all their tricks. I learned to handle my fists and took a heap o' beatings getting the lessons down right. For a year or so I followed the rodeos. That was for fun and *dinero,* but maybe that schooling will help too, when the rodeo comes off here. Maybe the Stormes'll smart some if Daw Reardon's son outrides their best! So that's the size of it. I've got to fight 'em — and whichever way they choose to fight, I'm ready!"

She raised her eyes and he was amazed to see tears laying upon her lashes. "You think a heap of the Stormes," he charged bitterly. "You're sorry that maybe things will be happening to them."

"I'm sorry — yes," she confessed. "But I'm sorry for the boy who never had a chance to be a boy. And I'm sorrier for the man who's trained himself for hating and killing, schooled himself to be a destroyer. Do you think your 'ghost lady' would have wanted it all to turn out this way? Do you think she got you out of harm's way so you'd come back someday with your heart full of hate? You've given me your answer, Steve. Good night."

She was out of the chair and through the doorway before he could raise a detaining hand. He sank back in amazement, wondering at the perversity of all women and of Sheila in particular. She liked him. The education of Stephen Reardon had included no study of women, yet he was sure of that. And yet, liking him, she could not endorse his cause. It was beyond his understanding.

The thought persisted that it was Tom Storme she was worrying about. Yet she had come to this very building where Tom was a prisoner and had not asked to see him. But that might have been because she wanted to spare him the humiliation of being seen in his present condition.

There was no knowing the truth and Steve was still brooding about it when he had a second visitor. This one was a man —

a little gray-headed oldster, his face the hue of old saddle leather, his wide friendly mouth half-hidden by a lyre-shaped moustache. He extended a horny hand.

"I'm Wash Winfield," he introduced himself. "I rod the Flyin' W at this end o' the valley and I'm sorta head o' the little fellers. I'm proud to cross palms with yuh, Reardon. I was in the Buckhorn when yuh trimmed Tom Storme down to his right size and I've been cravin' to speak to yuh since. Saw Doc Merritt's gal leave a spell ago, so I figgered yuh was alone. I'm here to tell yuh, yuh'll have the backin' of them that's suffered from the Sixty Six-Guns."

Steve instinctively liked this old cattleman, but he frowned at his words. "What kind of backing will that be?" he asked. "I had my hands full tonight, but there wasn't a man in sight until the fireworks was over."

"Yuh got a right to wonder why folks didn't give yuh a hand ag'in them hellions tonight," Winfield conceded. "Folks has been afraid of their shadders. The name o' Thunder Storme was enough to keep a man's gun pouched before, and the Sixty Six-Guns has made the odds twice as big. But with Jasper Galt to lend us *dinero* and yuh to show the way, things'll maybe be different. That show yuh put on tonight has made a lot of gents wonder what in hell excuse they ever had for callin' themselves men!"

Steve smiled. "I'm thankin' you," he said. "Maybe we'll clean out the carrion yet."

Old Wash nudged back his battered sombrero and scratched a bald spot. "Speakin' of carrion," he reflected, "I reckon the town'll have to bury that gunhog Tarn left behind."

Only then did Steve recall the flat-faced killer he'd shot from the saddle, for in the ensuing excitement and its aftermath he'd completely forgotten the fellow. With Wash Winfield bowlegging beside him, he crossed the silent street to where the man lay stretched, as hideous in death as he'd been in life.

Someone had hauled the body to the edge of the boardwalk and tossed a couple of sacks over it. Steve looked down upon the corpse. Here was a man who'd dealt in death and now those black wings had overtaken him. Yet he was entitled to burial.

"Seems like those that hired him should pay for his burying," Steve reflected aloud. "I'll take care of him, Wash. *Adios,* till the trails cross again."

As Winfield vanished into the darkness, Steve headed for the livery stable and got his own horse. He also fetched a pack-animal upon his return. Blindfolding the beast so that he might hoist the dead man across its back, he lashed the corpse there. Then, in the saddle, Steve headed out of Battleweed and up the valley, the pack horse trailing behind.

Little more than an hour before, Anse Tarn had dared Steve to enter the upper valley, threatening horrible punishment if Steve had the temerity to trespass. Steve was on his way to cross that devil's deadline. What was more, he was heading for the very stronghold of the Stormes.

five

Starkly outlined against the night sky, tremendous and awesome, the Bitter Root paced Steve as he led his grim cavalcade up Rearing Horse Valley. This was that wild, tumbled country where Montana thrust its timbered fingers into Idaho, a wilderness that might have been freshly wrought by the hand of God.

But Steve was blind to the beauty about him. Yonder, where the foothills were shapeless and shadowy as huddled worshipers kowtowing to the mightier peaks, was Dawson Reardon's old Rolling R spread. Mingled emotions rode in silent company with Steve, nostalgic memories choking him, carrying him back across the years to those long-gone days when this had been home.

Silence brooded upon the moon-mellowed land. No other living thing seemed to be abroad until, where the valley's walls began to pinch together, Steve came upon vast herds bearing the lightning-Slashed S brand of the Stormes, dark masses of cattle, dim and shapeless in the

66

distance. Riders guarded these cattle, their voices carrying to Steve as they sang to the bedded beasts, chanting soothing songs as old as the trail from Texas. Steve chose to give them a wide berth, circling warily to come at last to his trail's end.

A high wooden palisade of pointed logs crossed the narrowed valley here, a belligerent barrier. But beyond it the land tilted upward. A double row of cottonwoods climbed snakily from the palisade to form an avenue to the very door of Storme Castle, with that ungainly building visible from where Steve stood.

There was a certain weird beauty to the place, Steve acknowledged grudgingly. White precipices formed a backdrop for the structure and the moon washed it, casting an ethereal mist that clung like a silvery veil. Yet it was the house of Storme, and that, to Steve, invested it with a malevolent personality. Forty years ago Thunder Storme had built a frame house here, and as his brood increased through the years, he'd added wings haphazardly until the building sprawled to the four points of the compass. Beyond it and around it were barns and corrals and outhouses, marking the place for what it actually was, the headquarters of a mammoth cattle ranch.

Yet Steve, looking at it, saw it only as a citadel of evil, the palace of the power he had chosen to fight. Storme Castle. . . . Steve had read about castles when he'd pored over books in lonely snowbound line-camps. It would be fitting, and in keeping with the nature of the feudal lord who had built this one, Steve decided, if a dank moat surrounded Storme Castle, with a clanking drawbridge and a spiked portcullis to complete the picture.

For a long while Steve sat his saddle, eyeing it all. Overhead an owl, hunting, moved on silent wings, while a distant creek made fretful music in the night. But grim business had brought Steve here and he dragged his eyes away with an effort, for the place fascinated him as a snake fascinates a bird.

His first cue was to find a gate in the palisade and he began to skirt the upright logs in search of one. He headed in the right direction, as he shortly discovered, for a voice, challenging him from the shadows, gave proof of that.

"Where yuh figger yuh're goin', feller?" it wanted to know.

Steve, halting, peered hard and managed to make out a squat puncher, built along the general lines of a barrel, who lolled against

68

the gate, a cigarette dangling from his lips, a rifle cradled in his arms.

"Make any difference where a stranger rides hereabouts?" Steve asked blandly.

The sentry shifted his rifle as Steve slid from the saddle. "Stranger, eh?" the sentry said. "With the ranchers down yonder gettin' proddy, we don't cater to strange riders prowlin' around. Say! Ain't that a badge on yore shirt? What's yore name?"

Steve was surreptitiously edging toward the man. "Shucks, now," he said and laughed disarmingly. "Here's my calling card and —"

The sentry's eyes widened. "That pack-hoss of yourn! It's totin' a dead man!"

But Steve was close now — close enough. Too late the sentry realized there was something strangely amiss here and too late he tried to swing his rifle around. Steve was already presenting his calling card — an arcing fist that caromed off the squat puncher's jaw. The rifle went flying and the man, bouncing against the gate, slumped.

Instantly Steve was upon him, but the man had struck his head against the logs as he'd been slammed backwards and he'd struck hard enough to render him unconscious. Steve lashed the fellow's hands behind him with the sentry's own belt, then, surveying his handiwork, he saluted the still figure gravely.

"You work for 'em, son, and you're true to your salt," Steve said aloud. "Reckon that's as it should be. No hard feelings, feller. Maybe if we'd met some other place we'd have joshed and swapped the makin's and maybe sided each other if some trouble showed itself."

Then he pushed the gate inward and, mounting, rode between the cottonwoods to the very door of Storme Castle. The great house was wrapped in darkness, no single light showing, and the outhouses had no signs of life about them either. The castle didn't have the conventional gallery of a western ranch-house but was fronted instead by a great porch with towering pillars in the style of a Southern mansion. Steve deposited the body of the dead gunman upon the porch steps.

And there, his chore completed, a wild, reckless urge had its way with him, a need that grew until he could scarcely deny it. Why couldn't he enter the house? Why couldn't he seek out old Thunder, choke the truth out of him, make him name the man who had killed Daw Reardon?

Yet even as the desire blossomed, Steve fought it down. He'd been lucky this night, both in Battleweed and beyond it — too lucky. He'd gambled enough in his lifetime to know that good luck, crowded, sometimes boomeranged with disastrous results. Besides, such a showdown would be premature. First he had to humiliate the Stormes, drag them from their high seat. Gunsmoke would come later, the grand finale to a revenge long deferred.

Reluctantly he turned away to ride out to where the groaning sentry lay sprawled. The man was still unconscious but he was beginning to stir so Steve paused long enough to untie his hands. Then he went on down the valley. A grim satisfaction was his saddlemate on the trail back to Battleweed and he tumbled into bed in the marshal's quarters in the jail-building more than content with the course of events since he'd arrived in town.

He was up early the next morning, jerked from sleep by shouting at the far end of the street. But seeing the cause of the commotion as quickly as he stepped outside, he breakfasted first at Hop Gow's, then gravitated to the scene of the excitement, a peeled-pole corral near the rodeo grounds where a black, devil-eyed stallion lashed at the bars in magnificent fury while a crowd watched its antics from a safe distance.

Sheila was here, petite in riding garb. She returned Steve's smile as he singled her out.

"Never knew Satan had a colt," Steve remarked as he bent his gaze upon that snorting, lunging outlaw so intent upon wrecking the corral. He knew horses, did Steve, and here was one with the soul of a slayer.

Sheila shuddered. "That's Angelmaker," she explained. "He belongs to the Bar Star Bar in the lower valley and they bring him in every year for the rodeo. He ought to be shot! He's a killer and nobody's ever stayed the time limit with him. He's trampled two riders to death and crippled at least a half-a-dozen others. He hates everything human and he's growing more vicious and savage each year. Hate works two ways, Steve. It eats inward at the thing that fosters it."

Steve's mouth straightened. "I get the general idea," he said ruefully. "Me and Angelmaker, eh? Look at him there. Look at the devil shining in his eyes! I've never been afraid of a horse in my life, but I'm afraid of that one and I'm admittin' it. There's something about him that makes me want to be someplace else. But just the same, I reckon Angelmaker was just another colt a few years back, frisky as the rest and with all the makings of a good saddler. It was people that put the poison in him, made him over into the devil he is. Angelmaker wasn't just naturally full o' hate. Someone taught him to be that way!"

Her eyes clouded. "That's true," she admitted. "But just the same, Steve, he —"

Her words trailed away to nothing, for suddenly both of them were aware that something had gripped this crowd that thronged about the corral, something that silenced their noisy chatter as though the entire group had been stricken dumb, sending them shuffling to leave an open lane with Steve and Sheila anchored at its end.

Steve, an uncanny sensation tingling along his spine, swiveled his gaze, searching for the thing that was cowing the crowd. Six riders walked their horses toward them along one of the trails that led from the valley — but there were seven horses coming. And on the seventh, a pack-animal, was the lashed body of the gunman Steve had left at the door of Storme Castle.

"The Stormes!" Sheila whispered.

Steve didn't need to be told. He had forgotten many faces from the old days — Ernie Ide's and Hop Gow's and Jasper Galt's and Doc Merritt's among them — remembering them only when he'd seen them again last night. But not the Stormes. He

73

knew them instantly, the older ones, remembering them as though it were only yesterday that he'd been nine years old and had seen them ride the valley trails.

They were huge men, these Stormes, big and blond and built like Tom Storme. Three in the lead were middle-aged, and Steve knew at once that these were Noah, Nahum and Nathan, sons of old Thunder. The years had stooped them a little and etched lines in their ruddy faces, but he would have recognized them anywhere, these ogres of his boyhood. They sat their saddles now, looking like the wrath of God, their gaze haughty, their faces stern. They chose their own time to speak.

"You, with the badge," Noah Storme rumbled. "We've fetched back what you left at our door. Our man at the gate saw your badge, so it wasn't hard to figure out who'd come sneaking in the night. Anybody who wears a badge in Battleweed is Spider Galt's man. So are the Sixty Six-Guns, so that puts you in their class, mister. Bury your own dead!"

Here was effrontery that transcended effrontery and Steve could only laugh. "I don't blame you for not owning to that skunk you're packin'," he said mockingly. "But you don't expect anybody to swallow the part about the Sixty Six-Guns being on our side, do you?"

Another Storme pushed forward, a younger Storme, not much older than Tom, and at his side was a second, a brother, obviously, for the two were as alike as the holstered guns that swung from studded cartridge belts about their thick middles.

"Thaddeus and Theobald," Sheila whispered. "Twin sons of Noah."

"Don't waste talk on him, Paw," Thaddeus said hotly. "You know who he is, so you know why he's here. You knew it just as quick as one of our boys come lopin' from town last night with that yarn about how this gent beat up Tom. Lead language is the only kind he'll understand!"

Thaddeus Storme suited his action to his words by inching his fingers toward his gun, but his father restrained him with a gesture which Thaddeus sullenly obeyed. All that Steve saw. But now his eyes were on the sixth horseman and he started with recognition.

The horseman was big, bigger even than the Stormes, and obviously no kin of theirs. Shaggy of hair and beard, his eyes were brown and doglike beneath tufted eyebrows. He was a veritable giant, though his face was simple and childish, for he was

75

mentally deficient. Anyone could tell that at a glance. This was the Ox, long-time servant of the Stormes.

And seeing him again, Steve remembered this giant whom he'd failed to recall when Spider Galt had spoken of him, telling how the Ox had been the first to reach Dawson Reardon the night Steve's father had fallen.

Steve stared at the giant and it was like going back to a long-gone day, a day when the Ox had stopped at the Rolling R and produced a bag of peppermint candy which he'd shared with seven-year-old Steve. They'd played together that afternoon, finding a score of things to amuse the both of them, a child and a grown man whose mentality was like a child's. Dawson Reardon, finding the Ox there at sundown, had gently urged the giant to head home-ward and the Ox had left with many a back-ward glance.

Now Steve was seeing the Ox again and the Ox was staring too, his tufted brows knitted together. At last he grinned, a ges-ture vacuous yet friendly, contagious enough to make Steve grin in return.

"Howdy, Mister Reardon," the Ox boomed, encouraged apparently by that grin. "Ain't seen you or your little boy for quite a spell."

You or your little boy? That speech puzzled Steve until the truth behind it struck him. Time had no meaning whatsoever to the Ox. This simple soul thought that he, Steve, was Dawson Reardon, for he'd noticed the resemblance that had also impressed Doc Merritt. Steve framed the words of a friendly reply.

"Don't speak to him!" Theobald Storme snapped and the Ox lowered his shaggy head for all the world like a dog that has been reprimanded.

"We're not here to spout words, Reardon," Noah Storme said. "You've jailed Tom and your reasons for that act are obvious. Do you aim to turn him loose or do we have to tear your jail apart?"

"Seems like that's been tried, already," Steve observed drily. "And, by the way, where's Thunder? He's tin-god of Rearing Horse ain't he? Why isn't he here to welcome an old-timer home? Or maybe he's got reasons for not showing his face to a Reardon?"

"Thunder don't have to do any talking to your kind!" Nahum Storme spoke up. "We can say anything that needs to be said to you. Are you turning my son loose?"

Steve spread his legs apart, hooking one thumb near his holster. "You've barked and

77

that's all that's been needed to make folks jump pronto for a long time, ain't it, Stormes?" he observed. "But every dog sooner or later has his day. This valley's a powder-keg right now — and you damn well know it. Make another play at the jail like that one that was pulled last night, and it might be the spark to set it off. Is that what you want?"

Nahum Storme met Steve's gaze without flinching. "If something happened at the jail last night, we know nothing about it," he said. "We prefer peace to war. We always have. But it's probably wasted breath to tell you so. We'll be down here for the rodeo in a few days. Meantime, you'd better think things over."

He wheeled his horse and the others aped his action, the group stirring the dust of the trail as they headed up the valley again. The Ox lagged to the rear, ventured a backward glance and, finding himself undetected by his companions, also risked a friendly wave of one huge hand at Steve. Steve waved in return. Behind, the grim-burdened pack-horse stood with trailing reins. Sheila plucked at Steve's sleeve.

"They talked peace," she said. "Thaddeus had a chip on his shoulder but he's young and hotheaded. His father and his uncles were reasonable enough. Why couldn't you have come a step toward them?"

But Steve was scarcely listening, for his eyes were upon the departing Stormes, his lip curled. "They're coming to the rodeo," he ruminated aloud. "They're coming down to show us ordinary folks how to ride. They're coming to hog the show like they've hogged everything else. But maybe it'll be different this year. Maybe —"

She stamped her foot petulantly. "Of course it will be different," she flared. "Don't you know why Tom Storme was hanging around Battleweed instead of heading outside as he might have done? Tom should have hit the trail days ago, but he was waiting for the rodeo. Tom is their top rider, the best of the clan by far, and he's locked in your jail. It'll be easy for you to beat the others, Steve Reardon. But I — I hope you don't stand a show!"

She darted away, and Steve, his ears still ringing from her outburst, frowningly watched her go. Then, a decision made, he strode back to the jail-building, leading the pack-horse as far as the undertaker's on the way. In the jail, he found Tom Storme sitting up in his cell, vast bewilderment in his eyes.

"I can't figger it out," Tom said. "I remember gettin' a snootful and scrappin' with you last night. Then I remember guns bangin' hereabouts. Mind sayin' what it was all about."

"You don't have to figger it out," Steve snapped. "You've got thirty days to sit in here. But I hear tell you're the riding hope of the Stormes — the gent they pin their faith in. If you want the chance, I'll parole you on your word that you'll come back to jail. If you don't come, I'll drag you back even if I have to go into Storme Castle to collar you. Now get to hell out of here and get yourself in shape for the rodeo. I aim to have you at your best when I set out to beat you!"

six

Battleweed was aboil with excitement in the days that followed. The annual rodeo, Steve learned, had begun as a riding contest held among the ranchers to celebrate the end of the spring roundups. It had grown to become something of an institution in Rearing Horse and its date had been changed to the summer season, the show attracting spectators from all the Bitter Root, the crowds swelling to such proportions that it had been necessary to build a grandstand and bleachers on the outskirts of Battleweed.

During the last two years, with relations between the Stormes and the small ranchers growing more strained each day, the rodeo had become a sort of armed truce — a day set aside, when the only difference that mattered was between one man's saddle savvy and another's — personal differences being forgotten for the time.

The rodeo was a one-day affair, informal and irregular and bound only by the rules of fair play. A purse was made up by valley contributors, the prizes being big enough to inspire thirty-a-month cowhands to do their

81

best, yet not big enough to attract hordes of professional riders from beyond the horizons. A judge was imported from Hamilton to insure fair decisions and fractious horses were supplied by anyone who cared to bring them. Some of these buckers, like the dread Angelmaker, had earned reputations for devilishness that made them special attractions. The contestants acted as pickup men for each other.

The judge arrived the day before the rodeo, driving from Hamilton in a flashy buggy behind a team of fiddle-footed bays. Cow Rowley was his name. He was an old-timer in the Bitter Root, a retired cattleman who made a hobby of following the rodeos and was therefore considered to be something of an authority on matters pertaining to such shows. Also, he had an unquestioned reputation for honesty and both factions invariably accepted his decisions without argument.

He made his headquarters at the hotel, enthroning himself behind a pigeon-holed desk which was moved to his room; a gaunt, gray man, stern as justice itself but albeit a friendly fellow. It was one of his rules that all the participants register prior to the opening of the show and Steve, learning of this, went to the hotel room late that afternoon. Wash Winfield was there ahead of him and it was that old cowman, pumping Steve's hand vigorously, who introduced him to the rodeo judge.

"Reardon, eh?" Rowley said. "Seems like I once seed yuh at Pendleton at the big show."

"Might be," Steve smiled. "I followed 'em for a spell. Does that make any difference?"

"Reckon not," the judge said. "This here Battleweed show is supposed to be an amateur affair, but that don't mean it's just for younkers who never forked a cayuse before. If yuh used to be a professional, it don't make no never mind so long as yuh belong here now. We don't hanker to have professionals coming in just to pick up the prize money, so a gent's gotta be attached to this here range to qualify. What outfit do yuh belong to, Reardon?"

Steve flipped back his vest, revealing his badge. "No outfit," he said. "I'm town marshal here."

Cow Rowley frowned. "How come Dobe Kennedy ain't doin' the lawin', same as last year? How long yuh been totin' that badge?"

"About a week. Jasper Galt appointed me after Kennedy failed to do his duty in a little matter that came up one night."

"A week, eh?" Rowley mused. "Mister, I know Jasper Galt and I don't exactly call him a friend. But that ain't the point I'm gettin' at. I don't want to think that Galt gave yuh that badge to make it so's yuh could sign up for this here rodeo, him knowin' yuh was professional. I don't want to think that he's been bettin' on yuh, figgerin' to clean hisself up a pot full o' *dinero* when the drawings come off. But just the same, somethin' sorta stinks about this deal and I don't figger it would be right to let yuh register."

Steve was listening patiently enough, but as the import of Rowley's insinuation became clear, his wrath rose and with it a suspicion that the judge was barring him from the riding for a far different reason from the one Rowley had just put into words. "Now, listen — !" Steve began, but Wash Winfield laid a horny hand upon his arm.

"Easy, Steve," old Wash said soothingly. "Let me talk. Cow, yuh got this all wrong. This young gent is one of us, even though he ain't been hereabouts since he was a younker. He's the son of Daw Reardon who used to rod the Rolling R here in Rearing Horse."

"That don't spell nothin'," the judge said stubbornly. "It's him that's gonna do the ridin' — not his old man. I gotta have proof that he ain't just a gent that drifted in for the rodeo. Otherwise it smells like a frame-up to put a professional in for the prize money."

"It smells like a frame-up, all right," Steve blurted, his dark eyes blazing. "A dirty deal cooked up by the Stormes to keep me out of the saddle. But if you think for one minute, mister —"

Wash, who'd been tugging thoughtfully at his lyre-shaped moustache, interceded quickly. "Wait!" he cried. "I've got this thing figgered out. I reckon yore paw owned the Rolling R free and clear, Steve, and outside of the taxes which might be piled ag'in it since then, it's yourn. It was never put up for tax sale, I'm dang positive, because nobody's on it now. Yuh know where the papers are which proves it was yore paw's ranch and therefore yourn? I reckon if yuh're a ranch-owner in Rearing Horse, yuh're sure as hell entitled to ride in the Rearin' Horse rodeo. Ain't that right, judge?"

"It shore is right," Cow Rowley responded instantly. "Fact is, I couldn't stop yuh from enterin' then, even if I had a mind to. They ain't nothin' personal about this matter, son, and I've shore got nothin' ag'in you. I'm just lookin' out to be shore the show is on the square, which same is my job. Yuh show me the deed to the Rolling R and yuh're plumb eligible."

"But I can't show it to you," Steve groaned. "If there is a deed in existence, I don't know where it is. A copy of it would be on file at the court house in Hamilton, but there isn't time to get it. It would be past midnight before I could get to the county seat and I'd have to wait until the court house opened tomorrow mornin'. By the time I checked up and got back here, the rodeo would be over!"

He paused, his bitterness choking him. He *had* to ride in the rodeo. He'd counted so much on this chance to beat the Stormes and now he wasn't even going to be allowed to try. And then, in the depth of his despair, his eyes lighted with inspiration. "Shucks!" he chortled. "I know a gent who'd know all about a little thing like provin' ownership of a spread!"

It was Jasper Galt he had in mind. Galt operated the land office here in Battleweed and Galt, money lender and dealer in ranches, would probably know where the original deed might be found. He'd see Galt. Without further word he turned his back on the startled pair of oldsters and hurried out of the room and down the stairs to the street.

Galt's office wasn't far away. But Steve was doomed to disappointment when he reached it, for the little cubby-hole was locked and Galt was gone. Nor was he to be found at the bank or in the land office. A sleepy-eyed clerk in the latter place informed Steve that Galt had ridden into the valley on some business. The boss, it seemed, was appraising a lot of ranches these days.

Frustrated and angry at this turn of events which were like a devil's design to thwart him in his cherished hope, Steve paced the street aimlessly until he encountered Doc Merritt sauntering along, his black case in his hand.

"Maybe you're the man who can help me," Steve said breathlessly as he stopped the silver-maned old medico. Quickly he explained the situation "You were a friend of my dad's. Maybe you know whether he had a deed for the Rolling R — and where it would likely be now."

Doc Merritt stroked his chin thoughtfully. "Yes, Steve, there was a deed," he said. "And I know where it is. You see, Steve, I was out there the night — the night

87

of the trouble, like I once told you. It was a night when a doctor was sure needed and I aimed to help anybody who needed my help.

"But there was nothing I could do for Daw Reardon — except bury him. When the remnants of the little ranchers threw down their guns and surrendered, Thunder gave them until sunup to be out of the valley. I got one of them to knock a couple of packing cases into a coffin of sorts. It — it wasn't very fancy, Steve, but it was sturdy and it was the best we could do . . ."

"But the deed — ?" Steve persisted.

"It was in a tin box, setting on the table in the Rollin R ranch-house," Doc explained. "I saw it there before we laid your father away. That deed belonged to you, Stephen, but you were gone — nobody knew where. I figured some of the other ranchers, neighbors of Daw's, had slipped you away to safety. In any case, the paper had to be put in a safe place, kept for you."

"And you took it? You've got it now?" Steve asked eagerly.

"No, Steve. I wrapped that tin box to keep the weather from it and put it into the coffin with your father's body. Don't know why I did that instead of keeping it and taking it to my home. Some wild impulse, I guess — some feeling that Daw would want to be the caretaker of it until it could be given to you. It's in his coffin, Steve, where we buried him beside your mother out at the Rolling R."

Steve nodded, "I see," he said slowly. "It was as good a place as any, Doc, and it looks like I owe you for that, too, But now I've got to go after that deed."

"Wait!" Doc said quickly — too quickly. "That won't be necessary, Steve. I see you're determined to stay here in spite of my warning, and you're probably just as determined to ride in the rodeo. I'll talk to Cow Rowley and vouch for you. I've known him for years and I'm sure I can convince him that there's no question about whether you're the rightful owner of the Rolling R. You just wait here."

He whisked away and Steve watched him go, but Doc Merritt was no more than out of sight before Steve headed for the livery stable. He was convinced that Doc was his friend, even though that kindly medico was also a friend of the Stormes. Doc might plead Steve's case with Cow Rowley just as he'd promised to do, but Steve had a hunch that Doc's efforts would be wasted.

Cow Rowley was a stubborn old galoot. He hadn't listened to Wash Winfield's argument and it wasn't likely he'd listen to Doc Merritt. Cow Rowley wanted to see documentary proof and there was just one place to get it.

To accomplish his purpose, Steve needed several things — a shovel, a crowbar and a lantern. He managed to borrow all three articles, but there was something else he needed as well — a friend. He found Wash Winfield in the Buckhorn, which was overly crowded, the men who lined the bar talking of only one thing — the rodeo. Betting money was passing into the moon-faced barkeep's hands for safekeeping. At a nod from Steve, Wash detached himself from the crowd, followed him outside. The gray-headed oldster listened to Steve's story, then went for his horse without a word.

The sun was vanishing into the maw of the mountains as they put the town behind them and twilight spread its dusky mantle over Rearing Horse Valley as they veered toward the purpled blotch of the foothills, two men riding stirrup to stirrup, close to each other in the communion of silence. The miles were many and deep darkness had descended before they topped a low bluff and the buildings of the Rolling R sprawled below them.

"This is it," Wash announced.

Steve shrugged, not wishing to trust himself to words for he was feeling the sting of tears and was unashamed. Steve Reardon had come home at long last, for this was the place of his birth — or what was left of the place. Beneath yonder cottonwood, ghostly in the gloom, were the graves of his parents, and Steve headed directly to them. There they got the lantern aglow, playing the light upon the sunken, weed-grown mounds, the weather-faded headboards, tilting crazily. Wash dropped to his hands and knees and peered, his moustache almost brushing one grave-marker.

"Son, we've shore treed ourselves up a stump," he announced. "The letterin' was painted on these here timber tombstones and it's so faded yuh can't make it out. Ain't no way of knowin' which grave is which — unless you happen to remember."

"But I don't," Steve confessed, his voice low. "I remember Mother's grave of course. But Dad was buried afterwards. Doc Merrit would know, but —"

Wash scratched his bald spot. "Seems like it would be just as easy to dig into both graves as to head back to town and get the right of it from Doc," he observed. "Besides, there's a fifty-fifty chance that we'll be openin' the right grave the first try."

The old cowman's argument was logical enough and Steve stripped off his vest, tossed his sombrero aside and set to work with the shovel. Wash, standing near by, held the lantern aloft, splashing the light to the best advantage.

The ground was soft and Steve made the dirt fly as though he relished the task — which he didn't. There was something weird, unreal, about this thing he was doing and he wanted to get it over with as quickly as possible. It wasn't to his liking, for it gave him the feeling that he was some sort of ghoul, desecrating the resting place of his own parents.

Yet this thing he was doing was, indirectly, a blow against the Stormes; the only way he might prove his right to ride against them tomorrow. Daw Reardon would have wanted him to get into that contest regardless, Steve was sure. Daw Reardon, somewhere on that shadowy range beyond, would forgive him for this method he had to use to win his chance.

It was a comforting thought and it sustained him until the level of the ground was up to his armpits and the dirt was piled high and the shovel scraped against the wooden top of a coffin — a hollow, rasping sound. Then Steve pulled himself out of the grave.

"You'll savvy why I brought you along,

Wash," he said. "I'm askin' you to finish for me."

"I savvy," Wash said kindly. "They're yore paw and maw and it would likely be mighty hard for you when the lid's lifted. . . . Yuh just go take a stroll for yoreself, son. I'll finish up here and bring that paper to yuh."

Grateful beyond words, Steve thanked him with his eyes and marched off into the darkness. He found a grassy spot on top of the knoll and squatted there cross-legged, building a cigarette for himself and puffing at it thoughtfully as he stared off into the moonless dark.

He might have gone below and examined the buildings of the Rolling R, but there was no heart in him for such an investigation. He had a fair idea of what the years had done to them and he didn't care to see them as they would be. That would be as heart-breaking as seeing what was beneath that coffin lid. In his mind there was a picture of the old spread as he'd known it. He preferred to cling to that picture.

Memories . . . Once cattle had borne the brand of the Rolling R and the range had echoed to the rush and roar of roundup time. Smoke had risen from the branding fires near yonder corrals, now fallen into shapeless ruin. Calves had bawled and their mothers had grown frantic and a little boy had watched it all in wide-eyed wonder. Once people had lived below and their presence had changed a house into that magical thing — a home.

Summers — long, endless, lazy days, each of them an adventure in itself for a little boy. Winters, mild for Montana, here in the sheltered Bitter Root — a boy's excitement at the recurring miracle of snow — the weird tracings of frost's fingertips on a lonely ranch-house's windows. . . . Each of those memories was part of a lost heritage. This range would be stocked again, Steve vowed, but those other things were gone beyond recall.

He forced his mind to other thoughts and there was much to think about.

That attempt to murder him his first night in Battleweed, for instance. He'd suspected Dobe Kennedy at the time and he'd also suspected the Stormes. The fact that the Sixty Six-Guns had charged into town so soon afterwards put a different light on the matter.

Possibly one of them had been in the Buckhorn when he'd beaten Tom Storme. Possibly the fellow, true to those who paid him, had made his murder play and, when it had failed, had sought out Anse Tarn and the rest of the gunslingers and returned, only to fail again.

In any case it proved that death had once struck from the darkness and might be lurking under cover still, waiting another opportunity. His life was in danger, had been from the moment he'd been recognized in Battleweed. He walked with peril now and he'd have to be on guard constantly.

Thus he turned the matter over in his mind as he hunkered there, the sounds of night all about him, the stars beginning to appear, one by one, to rowel the dark curtain of the heavens. He didn't know how long he waited, but at last it occurred to him that Wash was taking an overly long time opening that coffin.

The lantern still glimmered yonderly like some sort of fallen star. Probably Wash was also sealing the coffin again and filling the grave, Steve decided, but he grew more restless as the minutes paced by. He was about to go and investigate when he saw the lantern bobbing toward him, cutting a swath of light before Wash's feet as the rancher bowlegged along.

"Was beginning to wonder what was keepin' you," Steve said.

"I had to open the other grave," Wash explained. "We picked the wrong one fust, but I figgered I could do the second job o' diggin'. Here's the tin box with the deed. It was buried with yore paw all right."

"Then let's be ridin'," Steve said and shivered. "I hanker to get out of here if the job's finished."

"Wait, Steve," Wash said and it came to Steve that there was something almighty wrong with the old rancher. It was Wash's voice that betrayed him, a hesitancy in his tone and a certain note of agitation that made Steve glance at him sharply.

"I ain't covered up yore maw's coffin yet," Wash went on. "They's . . . they's something I reckon you should see for yoreself . . ."

"What is it, man?" Steve demanded. "What's got you so excited?"

Without replying, Wash turned, beckoning with the lantern. Just as silently Steve followed him back to the grave that he, himself, had opened. Wash had removed the lid of the coffin. It was a crude affair, that coffin, and obviously Dawson Reardon had fashioned it by hand for the wife he'd lost, doing the best he could under the circumstances. But it wasn't the sight of his father's workmanship that made Steve stagger back to pass a hand before his unbelieving eyes.

The beam of the lantern shone directly into the coffin, the box that should be holding the remains of his mother, and there in the light the truth was undeniable. The coffin was empty.

seven

Rodeo Day. . . .

The morning sun climbed above Battleweed and the town sweated beneath it, a gay town bedecked with bunting and with a Fourth-of-July air about it, a town oblivious to the promise of blistering hours to come. The stands and bleachers were packed early and dust churned in the streets, as ranchers tooled their rigs through the milling throngs, their ginghamed wives beside them on buckboard seats, their children shrill and enthusiastic and freshly-scrubbed.

There was a parade of sorts to start things off. Old Cow Rowley led it, beaming and nodding to the crowd from his perch atop a flashy palomino, the contestants trailing behind him, a hastily-organized band bringing up the rear, blowing lustily at their instruments and making more noise than music.

Steve wasn't in the parade for he was out to the rodeo grounds early. The buckers were squealing in the corrals. Steve heard the thud of booted feet, saw sunlight mirrored in the sheen of horses, smelt the hot dust and reveled in those familiar things. Cheyenne, Pendleton, Calgary . . . the great shows — he'd seen them all. But for Steve there was a prize here for the taking that made this insignificant rodeo greater than any of them.

He'd proved his eligibility this morning, presenting the musty deed to the Rolling R to Cow Rowley and being promptly entered as a contestant. Now Steve was keeping his eyes peeled for Doc Merritt as the crowd surged into the stand and the bleachers.

Steve and Wash Winfield had re-buried that empty coffin out at the Rolling R last night and come to town, two perplexed men who had looked upon something that was beyond understanding. But Steve was remembering that Doc Merritt hadn't been eager to have him do any digging in the Rolling R cemetery. Had Doc known what Steve would find if the grave of Dawson Reardon's wife was opened first? Steve aimed to ask him.

But even the strange riddle of the Rolling R didn't seem important this morning. It was the rodeo that counted to Steve above all other things at the moment. Tom Storme had accepted his challenge. Steve was sure of that, for in the days since he'd paroled Tom, that youngster had stayed in Battleweed and had spent most of his time in a pitching saddle out here at the rodeo grounds. Tom was out to take the honors today — and Steve was here to beat him.

The Stormes were on hand to cheer their favorite, although they arrived too late for the parade. They rode in together, Noah and Nahum and Nathan and the twins, Thaddeus and Theobald, and the Ox, bedecked in a colored shirt, was with them, as excited as any child. A dozen Slashed-S cowpokes trailed behind. The Ox, spying Steve, grinned and waved his hand but Steve, his eyes peeled for the white-maned patriarch of the clan, saw that Thunder wasn't with them.

He wanted Thunder to be here today. He wanted Thunder in the stands when he beat Thunder's top-hand grandson. But if Thunder was here, he hadn't come with his family. Steve spied Spider Galt in the crowd, tall and stringy and conspicuous in rusty black where all else was color. Steve put a question to him.

"Thunder?" Galt repeated. "Let's see — he wasn't down to the rodeo last year and neither was Ophelia Storme, his missus. They're both pretty old folks now, you know, and maybe they're ailing. Some of the wives of the younger bunch came in a buggy a few minutes ago, but the two old folks weren't with them. But there's enough of the clan here to make it hot for you. Keep your eye peeled. I can savvy why you paroled Tom — but so can they."

With Wash Winfield, Steve also had words and that old cowman nodded sagely. "Shore, Steve, we'll all be watchin' yore back, every last one o' us little fellers," he promised. "With them Sixty Six-Guns raisin' hell, folks is mighty proddy ag'in the Stormes and we won't be takin' no chances. But so long as they behave themselves, it's their rodeo just as much as ourn."

Steve looked for the Sixty Six-Guns among the crowd. That was wasted effort, for it dawned upon him that the only one he could recognize on sight was Anse Tarn.

If the wolf-pack had drifted into town by twos and threes they might easily have been absorbed, undetected, by the milling throng. All of those gun-slingers might be in the stands, but there was no way of knowing if they were. But the rodeo was getting underway and Steve forgot the personal danger that might be shadowing him in his zest for the things to come.

The morning was given to bulldogging

and roping and steer-riding, the things calculated to entertain the crowd. Steve had a
hand in all these events, rolling up his share
of points, recognizing the familiar smells of
dust and sweat and enjoying himself after a
fashion.

He was adept enough with catch rope and
pigging string to make a showing but he entered each doing mechanically with a
growing impatience for the riding contests
to come. These would be the main events,
the ones that would count, the ones that
would decide who was winner of this rodeo.
For Steve, these other events were only a
period of waiting, a time of dragging suspense.

Tom Storme, his checkerboard shirt and
fancy neckerchief fitting garb today, was
into the thick of the morning's doings as
were the twins, Thaddeus and Theobald,
and Nathan Storme, youngest of Thunder's
three sons. A half dozen of the Slashed-S
riders participated too, including the squat
little puncher who had guarded the gate the
night Steve had managed to reach the door
of Storme Castle. The fellow recognized
Steve too, but the puncher contented himself with a long, hard stare, remembering,
apparently, that this was a time of truce. All
of the Slashed-S bunch made good show-

ings. But it was the afternoon that was going to decide the issue.

The brassy sun climbed overhead, then arced from zenith toward the west. There was a brief intermission for lunch. Only a portion of the crowd left the stands, since most of the ranchers' wives had brought along boxes of food.

Steve sauntered down to Hop Gow's, finding that place packed to the doorway, and bolted his food with a gnawing impatience that manifested itself in his lengthened stride as he hurried back to the arena. With the bucking contests about to begin, he was one of the first to crowd to the judge's stand to draw a folded slip of paper from a filled sombrero.

Tom Storme was here too, and others as well. Steve, seeing riders unfold their slips hesitantly and peek at the name of the horse each had drawn, recognized their fear, for he shared it with them. Angelmaker . . .

No man was anxious to ride that devil-horse. The barkeep from the Buckhorn, un-official stakeholder, was here; resplendent in a derby and flowered vest that looked as out of place on him as a saddle on a steer. Leaning from the stand, he summed up the situation quickly enough.

"Bettin' odds are even between any horse

in the bunch and the man that picks it," he said, "unless that horse is Angelmaker. In that case it's ten to one — on the hoss!"

But now there was a commotion at the chute and things were underway. A leather-lunged announcer had come up from Hamilton and the fellow was really warming to his work. "Dishrag Condon of the Two Bar Two," he bellowed. "Coming out on Steamboat!"

That was the beginning. The Two Bar Two peeler, a lanky whiplash of a cowpoke, erupted from the chute to absorb four seconds of sunfishing dished out by a showy bay that was an equine contortionist. It was a good fight while it lasted, but it didn't last long. Steamboat sent Dishrag Condon sailing skyward to sprawl on all fours in the dust. Steve, as pickup man, edged in to get the bay's reins while the crowd voiced its appreciation in a united howl.

That howl echoed and re-echoed at the next announcement for Tom Storme came out on Jawbreaker, a stringy gelding who looked as stiff as saddle leather but who proved to be as pliant as sword steel. The mount proceeded to turn himself inside out, but Tom stuck.

Steve, his sombrero pulled low, his eyes squinted against the sun, watched and knew he was watching a rider. There was no doubt about that. Tom Storme had what it took. There was show and flash to his riding, things calculated to win a crowd's approval. And the fellow had a natural sense of balance and a touch of the professional in the way he handled his horse. He piled up points for himself before the timer's whistle signaled the finish.

Steve came out next, straddling a wiry black. His first seconds in the saddle told Steve that the creature was no bucker. He'd drawn an easy mount, but this sort of good luck was bad luck for Steve. With the skill that was his, he got the black to pitching. He wanted that horse to look like an insane thing, a creature of fury, and he succeeded. It was a showy ride and it looked like the real thing to the stands, for the crowd was wild when he finished.

Old Wash slapped Steve's back. "Listen to 'em!" he chortled. "They're goin' plumb loco. They're finally seein' a show that ain't a one-man show. Rearin' Hoss has found out that somebody else can ride besides Tom Storme!"

Steve, nodding, knew that was just about the way it was. Thaddeus Storme had a turn on a buckskin called Badman, but Tom's cousin proved to be only a fair rider. He was good enough to take his turn, but he wasn't good enough to stick for the finals. The contest was between a young gent with blue-black hair and another young gent, blonde and ruddy — Steve Reardon and Tom Storme.

The first round of riding proved it and every man in the stands was aware of the truth. There was a new rush of betting to keep the bartender busy. Steve knew what those bets were about. It had been man against horse when the money was laid on the line before. Now it was man against man.

Tom Storme, in the next drawing, got a sand-colored hellion that could have taught Jawbreaker a dozen tricks and still had a dozen to spare. He was tough, that horse, and just as powerful as he was showy. Yet Tom put up a winning ride — a ride that Steve had to sweat to duplicate when he exploded out of the chute on a hammer-headed gelding that leaped like lightning and landed like a rock. He gave Steve a few bad moments at the start, but Steve rose to the test, gritting his teeth and riding that four-legged piledriver to the whistle and beyond it.

And so the long afternoon passed, the dust boiling in the arena, the crowd shouting itself hoarse. There were more drawings. There was more punishment. The sun spent itself and slanted toward the Bitter Root, trailing lengthy shadows across the arena.

The endless day was nearly done and Steve was one vast ache, his wounded shoulder throbbing, but still there was a fierce exultation in his soul that was a balm in itself. He'd outridden Tom Storme every step of the way. He'd conquered and the proof of it was in the disgruntled faces of the Stormes who were in the arena.

Yet there had to be a last ride — a deciding ride. Two men had pulled through the bucking finals and those two were Tom Storme and Steve Reardon. And Tom, making his last drawing, put his heart and soul into the ride, a dangerous one, and stayed until the whistle.

That alone was enough to stiffen Steve's spine, to fill him with a grim determination, as he crossed to the judge's stand and selected one of the few slips still left in Cow Rowley's big sombrero. The stands were breathless now, knowing the significance of this moment. And in that hushed silence with a thousand eyes upon him, Steve unfolded his slip and glanced at the name that was written upon it.

Then he was raising his eyes, staring into the face of the judge. Yesterday he'd crossed with this stubborn old man, and because Cow Rowley had been reluctant about entering him in the rodeo, Steve had suspected that Rowley was working hand-in-glove with the Stormes. Afterwards he'd known those suspicions were ridiculous and he'd felt a little foolish for harboring them. Today, at this incredible moment, his suspicions were born anew, rising phoenix-like from their own ashes. But there was no guile, no sign of treachery in the seamed face of Cow Rowley.

Shrugging, Steve passed back the slip, headed toward the chute. No, Cow Rowley was an honest man and it was malignant fate that was conspiring against Steve. The stands were roaring with one throaty bellowing voice, for every man was on his feet as the announcer, too excited to wait until Steve was in the saddle, shouted through his megaphone, his stentorian tones echoing across the arena.

"Steve Reardon, folks! He's done some mighty nice ridin' today. If he can stick with this one he'll be the winner for sure. A top-hand rider on a top-hand hoss, folks. *Steve Reardon of the Rolling R — comin' out — on Angelmaker!*"

eight

Angelmaker! That unridden killer-horse . . . !

Truly fate had stacked the cards against Steve to rob him of the victory he'd spent a heart-breaking, back-breaking day to earn.

The day he'd first set eyes upon Angelmaker, he'd told Sheila that he'd never been afraid of a horse in his life, but he'd admitted that he was afraid of Angelmaker. It was the truth and he wasn't ashamed of it, for the horse had the look of Lucifer. Yet Steve had drawn him and he didn't doubt the fairness of the drawing. The cards had fallen against him, that was all. His rocky jaw tight, he girded himself for the battle to come.

Angelmaker was girding himself as well. In the corral where the stallion had waited, he'd fought like seven devils against the saddle and had to be thrown before the hull could be put into place. He gave six sweating, livid-faced cowpokes a furious five minutes before they got him into the chute, but once between the bars the horse stood there, trembling and snorting. Angelmaker was far too cagy to waste strength fighting the chute. He was a veteran at this sort of thing and he knew what was coming.

Pausing on the chute's bar for an added second of rest, Steve swept his eyes across the sea of faces in the stands. This was his moment, but there was nothing of triumph in it. His friends were there — the small ranchers who might look upon him as their leader just as other small ranchers had followed the lead of his sire in the past. And his enemies were there, too — the Stormes, who would be anticipating his defeat. Possibly old Thunder himself was among them.

Steve grinned, the gesture humorless and tight. He eased over into the saddle and Angelmaker flinched beneath him. The leather-lunged announcer made his speech all over again. Steve tugged his sombrero low and slid his feet into the stirrups and nodded to the tense cowpuncher at the gate.

In the deathly stillness that followed, the creak of the gate was like the crack of doom and Angelmaker leaped out like unleashed lightning, bucking awkwardly at first, yet with dynamiting force. Here was a creature with a natural hatred for the saddle and a natural instinct for finding ways to vent that hatred.

It was going to be bad — mighty bad.

Pendleton . . . Cheyenne . . . Calgary . . . Steve Reardon had ridden in those shows, but he'd never ridden anything like this hell-sired horseflesh beneath him now.

From awkward bucking, Angelmaker went into systematic sunfishing, twirling top-like when he hit, a nauseating motion that snapped Steve's head like a whip end. Then — abruptly — Angelmaker changed his tactics. Trumpeting shrilly, he charged across the arena at a furious speed, only to plow the dust with his front hoofs, raising choking clouds that blinded Steve and left him gasping.

It was an old trick, this coming to a sudden stop, and Steve braced himself for it. But Angelmaker had made a new trick out of an old one. With the fence just ahead, the horse spun instead of stopping, scraped against the barrier. Steve might have been torn from the saddle and it was pure instinct that warned him in time to kick free from one of the stirrups, throw himself out of danger.

Instantly Angelmaker went down and rolled only to lurch up again. But swift as the devil-horse was, Steve was swifter, getting out of the saddle and back into it with perfect timing. Angelmaker immediately went into his bucking act again, heaving skyward, twisting and turning and landing like a crashing boulder.

The crowd was on its feet, wild with excitement, shouting hoarsely. Steve didn't hear them. He couldn't hear anything but the pounding of blood in his own ears, the *thud — thud — thud* of hoofs striking the ground. A dozen times instinctive balancing saved him. A dozen times he was certain that he was going to be unseated, could even vision himself upon the ground, flailing hoofs lashing at him. Two riders had been killed by this horse and a half-dozen others had been crippled. Would today see another victim added to that grisly list?

Trick and countertrick — horse against man — dust in his nostrils and the salty taste of blood upon his lips . . . He had been riding this horse forever. He had been in this pitching, tossing hurricane-deck of a saddle since the beginning of time. He was doomed to stay here forever, to go through an eternity of whirling sky and swaying ground.

But someone was blowing a whistle. It shrilled again and again, an incessant thing that rasped at Steve's nerves as a file rasps upon steel. And then it seeped into his foggy consciousness that it was the timer's whistle he was hearing. He'd won! He'd ridden Angelmaker!

It was a thought that beat like a ceaseless drum through Steve's muddled senses. He'd won! He'd won! And that was when the saddle girth snapped. Steve felt the hull slipping even before he understood exactly what had happened and he kicked free automatically, leaped to the ground, landing sprawling. Even then he wasn't alert to danger. He saw Noah Storme, the nearest pickup man, spurring toward him, his face twisted with mingled emotions.

"I won! I'm champion!" Steve babbled, trying to focus his eyes on his enemy's face. "Ask old Thunder how he likes that! Ask him —"

The shrill trumpeting of Angelmaker jerked him around. The horse was rearing, his great body blotting out the setting sun, a menacing monster with murderous hoofs poised. Instinctively Steve threw up an arm to protect himself — a gesture as futile as trying to stop a torrent with a straw.

He was doomed, but even then he was still too groggy to realize fully his own danger. He only knew he had ridden Angelmaker to the whistle and then the saddle girth had given away. A gun roared almost in his ear. He smelled the acrid tang of powdersmoke, felt hands jerking him aside. Angelmaker was stretched upon the ground kicking — a killer horse who would kill no more.

Then Steve began to understand, the red mist fading from his brain. He'd ridden Angelmaker and won the rodeo. He'd outridden Tom Storme after drawing the worst bucker this range could supply. But his victory was like ashes in his mouth, for now he knew that he owed his life to Noah Storme who had put a bullet into Angelmaker and dragged Steve out of the way in the very nick of time.

What did a fellow say when he hated a man and that man had just saved his life? "I'm — I'm thankin' you plenty," Steve managed to blurt, but Noah Storme didn't hear him, for Thunder's son was already turning his back upon Steve.

Shrugging, Steve limped away, oblivious to the roaring crowd whose clamor drowned the announcer's superfluous attempt to name the winner of the rodeo. A suspicion was festering within Steve and he approached the dead horse and examined the wrecked saddle. Then Steve headed toward the chute with deadly directness and there he found a dozen men loitering, Spider Galt among them.

"A grand ride!" Galt applauded, his bony face beaming. "A grand victory! This will bolster the morale of the ranchers like nothing before it. They've found that the Stormes can be beaten at the rodeo and they'll realize they can be beaten in the valley as well. A dozen little fellows have been in to borrow money for guns and powder. There'll be a dozen more tomorrow after this lesson sinks in —"

"Galt," Steve interjected grimly as he took the boss of Battleweed aside, "there's been two undercover tries at killing me lately. The first was the night I jailed Tom Storme. The second was today — now! Somebody used a knife on that saddle! It was fixed so that a certain amount of strain would finish the job. You can see it for yourself."

"Fixed the saddle!" Galt gasped, and his eyes narrowed thoughtfully. "Hell, a dozen men might have done it. There were plenty of them around the saddles today and in the finals, when it boiled down to you and Tom Storme, every eye was on the arena. But wait! The Ox was hanging around the gear not half an hour ago! And he had a knife in his hand, was whittling away at a stick of wood!"

"The Ox! I can't believe it! Do you figger the Stormes put him up to it? But shucks, Noah Storme saved my bacon when the saddle did let go. If it hadn't been for him, I'd be dead now."

"What else could he do?" Galt observed acidly. "They must have figured Angel-maker would make a quick job of you, once you were on the ground. Angelmaker was hopping all over the arena and it was just Noah's bad luck that he had to be handy when you finally fell. With it working out that way, he had no choice but to make a play at saving you — in order to save himself. If he'd stood by and let the horse get you, folks would have savvied right now what was going on and torn him to pieces!"

Steve jerked around and eyed the crowd, a deadly anger fermenting within him. The stands were emptying already, for the show was over save for the presentation of the prize money and many of the spectators had long ways to go. Funnels of dust lay along a half-dozen different trails from town. Grouped together, the Stormes and their riders were taking their own way, heading toward the upper valley. All except Tom Storme. He was still here, elbowing his way through the crowd, striding purposefully toward Steve.

"I know who you are now, Reardon," Tom said. "My folks had a chance to tell me today. They wanted me to ride home with them, and maybe if I had any sense I'd be on the trail right now. But you turned me loose on my word so I'd have a chance to be ready for today. And then you outrode me fair and square. Take me to your damn jail, Reardon, and get it over with!"

But Steve scarcely heard him, for Steve was already racing toward his own horse. Over his shoulder he flung words to Spider Galt. "The cell keys are in my desk," he cried. "Lock him up for me and see that he gets some supper, will you? I'm going to be right busy. Maybe I'm bitin' off more than I can chew, but I aim to try and have another of his outfit in jail tonight to keep him company — the gent that's handy with a knife. The charge'll be attempted murder!"

Yonder, Cow Rowley was waving the prize money, beckoning to Steve, but that presentation was going to have to wait. For Steve, piling into his saddle, was neck-reining out of the arena to beeline after the Stormes.

nine

Leaning low over his saddlehorn, thundering out of Battleweed on the trail of the Stormes, Steve was sure he could overtake them easily enough. They'd used their horses for pickup work at the rodeo and those mounts were tired. So was Steve's for exactly the same reason, but that only evened things and the Stormes would be taking their time. Granting that they'd engineered the fixing of Angelmaker's saddle — and Steve was positive that they'd had a hand in that unsavory business — they'd be feeling reasonably secure, since they hadn't been challenged in the arena. Consequently they wouldn't hurry, nor would they be expecting pursuit.

Yet Steve couldn't help but wonder if he was taking the trail to boothill as he cut the breeze out of town. Wrath had sent him on this chase, a fierce anger that demanded nothing less than the arrest of the Ox, but with the first flame of it dying before the cold wind of reason, he reined in his horse to a walk.

There were certain factors he had to consider. He'd bested the Stormes today, beaten them before the rodeo crowd. He'd survived in spite of the attempt that had been made upon his life. And Tom Storme's peculiar code had given the family a second defeat, for Tom had chosen to return to jail when he might have broken his word and ridden away with his clan. Those things had undoubtedly put the Stormes in an ugly mood. Snatching the Ox from them was liable to be no simple matter, a task that would probably end in gunsmoke, with un-beatable odds stacked against Steve.

But Steve had no thought of forgetting the matter. He merely intended to be cautious so he trailed the group furtively, staying behind them while the trail led deeper into the valley and the sun surrendered to the crowding dusk and the shadow legions came to weave their purple mantle.

The way became a lonely one as the miles unreeled, for other riders had branched off below Battleweed. Steve was getting deeper into Storme country. The shrubbery became thicker — service-berry bushes and clustering rose briar with a few scraggly fir trees scattered here and there. Eyeing the surroundings speculatively, Steve spurred ahead in a wide semi-circle, skirting the Stormes, until he reached a spot admirably suited for a purpose he had in mind — a clump of bushes.

Deep darkness offered concealment enough, but he forced his horse into the bushes to be on the safe side. And here he sat his saddle, a gun in one hand, his other hand clamped over his mount's nostrils, his ears tuned for the beat of hoofs that would tell him the Stormes were coming. He didn't have long to wait. Horsemen took shape in the night and Steve nudged his mount into the open.

"Sky 'em!" he ordered.

They hoisted their hands. They had no choice, for Steve had taken them completely by surprise and the gun in his hand never wavered. Their astonishment was ludicrous, but Steve didn't smile at the sight of those sagging jaws. Instead, his leveled gaze locked with the icy blue eyes of Noah Storme.

"You saved my life today," Steve said evenly. "I might be owin' you something for that if it wasn't for the fact that another of your bunch pulled a stunt that cancels what you did. I reckon you know what I mean. The Ox is under arrest. As marshal of Battleweed, I'm taking him back with me, savvy? Move over here, Ox."

"Listen!" young Thaddeus Storme interjected before his father could speak. "I don't know what your game is this time — but I don't like it! What you got against the Ox? If this big feller has done anything wrong, spill it! You've been around here long enough to know we do our own lawin', Reardon. I give you the word of a Storme that he'll get a trial when he gets home and he'll be punished if he's done anything to be punished for."

Steve laughed. "The word of a Storme!" he mimicked. "I'm granting that Tom kept his word to me, but that was only a little matter involvin' about three more weeks in the calaboose. This is a heap different. For what the Ox did, you'd probably buy him a new pair of boots or another fancy shirt. To hell with your kind of law!"

Cursing, Thaddeus Storme went for his gun, his hand plummeting downward. He was fast enough but it was a foolish move for Steve's iron was already in his hand and it bucked and spat fire now. Noah's son, groaning, clutched at his arm, blood seeping between his fingers as his gun fell to the trail. Instantly Steve's gun was swiveling, sweeping the group, discouraging anyone else who might happen to be planning a like move.

"Over here, Ox," Steve snapped. "You're going back to town with me!"

It was obvious that most of this was beyond the Ox's understanding, but he came, his shaggy face knotted in bewilderment, his great head wagging. Grasping the giant's reins with his free hand, Steve maneuvered around the group and cautiously backed down the trail, his gun still covering the silent, sullen clan.

The shrubbery was even thicker here and Steve was soon out of sight. He put spurs to his horse then, jerking the Ox's mount into a gallop, but only for a distance. Yonder a bush-mottled slope tilted upward and Steve climbed it, seeking cover and forcing the puzzled Ox to ape his actions. The ruse brought its own reward a moment later when the Stormes thundered past, angry faces bent low over saddlehorns as they plied spurs and quirts recklessly.

Steve chuckled. "Look at 'em," he reflected aloud. "So dang mad they're not even taking time to cut sign. Wait'll Thunder hears about this!"

With the hoofbeats growing dimmer in the distance, he loped off at an angle, his prisoner with him. Riding along, Steve eyed the Ox speculatively. The giant carried a gun which Steve immediately transferred to his belt, still holding his own weapon at the same time. The strength of six men was probably packed into the giant's big carcass and the moods of the Ox were bound to be uncertain things.

"You can lower your hands," Steve told him. "But behave yourself, savvy?"

The Ox's arms slumped and he immediately pawed into a pocket of the fancy shirt he wore. Instantly Steve, alert to danger, tilted his gun, his finger tensing on the trigger. But the giant, pulling a crumpled paper sack into view, extended it, his face wreathed in that friendly, vacuous grin of his.

"It's good," the Ox explained eagerly. "Yuh like it? Yuh just put some in yore pocket and take it home to yore little boy. Will you do that, huh? It's good. It's peppermint candy."

Peppermint candy!

Slowly Steve pouched his gun, avoiding the Ox's eyes as he did so. For at this moment Steve knew Spider Galt's suspicions had been foolish — and this chase had been just as foolish.

The Ox hadn't tinkered with Angelmaker's saddle. The Ox didn't have intelligence enough for such a trick, even if the Stormes coached him. And looking at the Ox now, seeing him with that ridiculous paper bag extended, his doglike eyes glowing in his eagerness to be friendly, Steve was heartily ashamed of himself. This giant who had once brought peppermint candy to a little boy didn't have an ounce of maliciousness in his whole big body.

Steve absently took some of the candy, nudging back his sombrero and tugging at one blue-black lock in perplexity while he crunched the confection.

What to do with the big fellow? Turn him loose and head him toward Storme Castle? Steve didn't know — but he knew he could no more jail the Ox than he could kick a dog just because that dog happened to give its devotion to the Stormes. Yet he remembered a question he'd once put to Spider Galt — and the man's reply.

". . . I was with the small ranchers that night, but I wasn't with your father when he fell," Galt had said. "It was the Ox who picked him up. I guess the big galoot couldn't tell a Storme from an enemy."

Here was the fellow who might be able to name the one man Steve sought above all others. But could the Ox remember the killer of Dawson Reardon? Could he name him? Steve eyed the giant thoughtfully.

"You remember me and my little boy," Steve said urgently. "Now think hard — real hard. Do you remember the night when the

Stormes came to our place a-gunnin'? Do you remember me gettin' hit, wounded bad?"

Even as he spoke, Steve wondered if he was overdoing it. Twice the Ox had indicated that he'd mistaken Steve for Dawson Reardon. But was he, Steve, only reminding the Ox that Dawson Reardon was dead and that he was the son, not the father? Who could guess at the workings of the weakened mind behind those shaggy brows?

The Ox only wrinkled his forehead and wagged his great head, patently confused. Then, seeing Steve's chagrin — "I can wiggle my ears!" the Ox announced jubilantly and demonstrated. "Can you?"

Steve bit his lip in disappointment and gave himself to reflection. So far he'd drawn deuces, but there still might be a mine of information stored in the Ox's shaggy head. But how to unlock it?

"Come on," said Steve. "We're ridin'."

The Ox obediently followed while Steve led the way, a wild scheme shaping itself as he loped along. They rode in silence, heading toward the foothills while the moon, big and benign, climbed above the distant Sapphire range to the east. Steve picked the way cautiously, choosing rocky ground wherever he could find it, splashing up a creek for a distance, doing everything to cover his trail, mindful that the Stormes would shortly realize they'd been duped and would be looking for him.

But all this was done mechanically. Steve, deep in thought, was hoping against hope. Could he fan the spark of forgotten memory in the Ox's mind? The more he thought about it, the more the scheme he'd concocted seemed utterly fantastic. But it was worth a try. There was everything to win and nothing to lose.

Presently they were topping that low bluff where Steve had hunkered the night before, and a moon-drenched huddle of buildings spread below them — The Rolling R.

Last night Steve had chosen not to look upon the wreckage that was here, but tonight he had no choice if he was to accomplish his purpose. Things were as he'd expected them to be and there was nothing but heartbreak here. The glass was long gone from the windows of the little house Dawson Reardon had built for his bride — the house that had been Steve's birthplace. The doors sagged on their leather hinges, the yard was weed-choked and littered with debris and the corrals were sprawling despondent things and the barn a wind-scarred ruin.

For a long time Steve sat his saddle, looking down upon this place that had once known the echo of a woman's laughter, the shrill shouts of a little boy at play. Then, his rocky chin firm, he headed down the slope, the Ox following him. Dismounting, Steve hunkered in the shadows before the house, the Ox squatting at his side. Without a word, Steve watched the Ox studiously as the big fellow eyed his surroundings with a growing interest. Finally Steve pointed above.

"Can you see 'em?" he hissed. "Men are up there, hiding on the bluff — the Stormes and their riders! There'll be guns popping and plenty of trouble!"

He paused then, his eyes on the Ox, and Steve almost stopped breathing as he watched for some sort of reaction from the giant. The Ox knotted his broad face, his eyes twin pools of puzzlement. Had those words meant anything to him?

"There's gotta be a fight . . ." the Ox said slowly. "Thunder says there ain't no chance no more . . . It's bad . . . bad . . ."

Exultation flooded Steve, a sense of success so heady as to leave him almost dizzy. It was working! The Ox had proved that time had no meaning to him. Twice he'd mistaken Steve for Dawson Reardon. Steve had deliberately brought him here, fetched him to the Rolling R with the mad hope that seeing the setting of that killing of long ago might reawaken the Ox's memory. Now Steve was making the Ox believe that time had turned backward and this was that blazing night of bloodshed. Could he make the Ox relive that night as well?

"They're shootin'! Can't you hear 'em?" Steve exclaimed. "They've got us ringed! We gotta make our last stand here, gents. There's hell to pay. Look . . . !"

It was insane. It was unreal, stagey, an eerie farce that sent shivers along Steve's spine. Up yonder there was nothing but silence and shadows, yet Steve was peopling the bluff from his imagination, peopling it from the fragmentary stories he had heard about the showdown that had taken place here, and from memories that were seared into his childish mind fifteen long years ago.

But could he make the Ox see those ghosts of yesterday? Would the Ox speak even if his memory was jarred? The giant was trembling with excitement, his broad forehead corrugated. And suddenly he cried out as though in pain.

"Men's dyin'!" he shouted. "Men's sprawlin' all over the place. It's awful . . ."

And Steve, knowing that the impossible

might be possible, knowing this wild scheme of his stood a chance of success, came to his feet, fighting to bridle the excitement that surged through him. "I'm gonna give 'em hell," he shouted. "I'm gonna give 'em lead for lead. Come on! Are you gents with me?"

"Wait!" the Ox bellowed. He too had come to his feet and now he was glaring about wildly, his eyes searching the shadows around the house. "The boy! The little boy! He's down here! I saw him from the top of the bluff. He'll get hisself killed with all this lead bein' tossed around. I've come to get him! Where is he?"

So that was why the Ox had been among the enemies of the Stormes that night! That's why he'd been near enough to be the first man to reach Dawson Reardon when he'd fallen! And now the Ox had returned to yesteryear. He was remembering! And Steve was going to make him remember the rest of it.

He didn't answer the giant's frantic questions. Instead, Steve sped across the weed-choked yard, his gun spitting fire, driving bullets at the sky and into the ground. He might have been a man berserk. He might have been launching himself against the devil's own legions from the look of him.

But a dozen paces from the house he spun and dropped to the ground with a howl of anguish as though a bullet had found his vitals.

Step by step he'd built toward this moment. Step by step he'd played this desperate farce. Here was the curtain act for the fantasy — the encore designed to wring a name from the Ox. With his nose in the dirt, Steve lay there listening to the clamor of his own heart, listening for some sound from the Ox, wondering through endless seconds whether the Ox would respond as he hoped the giant would. Then heavy boots thudded and the Ox, his broad face twitching, was beside Steve, cradling him in his arms.

"Yuh're shot . . . yuh're bleedin'!" the Ox moaned. "Don't die . . . don't die . . ."

"I'm finished," Steve gasped. "Which one of 'em got me? Which one of 'em pulled the trigger? They're your friends, Ox — I know that. But before I cash in my chips, tell me . . ."

Tears were rolling down the Ox's cheeks, worming their way through his shaggy beard while his great body shook with sobs. The Ox, creature of kindness, couldn't stand the sight of suffering. Back across the years he'd gone, back to the turmoil and anguish that must have twisted his simple soul that hellish night. "Shot yuh in the back," the Ox cried. "That's what he did . . ."

"*Who*, Ox?"

"I saw him," the Ox said numbly. "Shot yuh in the back . . ."

"*Who?*"

But the Ox had given way to an uncontrollable grief, a grief so deep as to leave him wordless, a genuine grief. It was maddening for Steve, lying there in the big fellow's cradling arms, knowing that a word or two would give him the name he wanted so desperately. Yet he had to play his cards cautiously. He had to maintain this deception and to force matters might be to break the spell, to snatch the Ox out of the past and into the present.

"It's gettin' dark," Steve groaned. "I'm goin' . . . goin' fast. Tell me his name, Ox. Let me know . . . before it's . . . too late —"

"I'll tell yuh," the Ox said fiercely, and then Steve heard the waspish buzz of a bullet, so close that the lead drew blood from the lobe of his ear and plowed a bloody furrow across the muscles of the Ox's cradling arm. Far up the slope a gun burned a hole in the night. And Steve instantly forgot that he was impersonating a dying man as he flung himself aside, rolled, came to his feet with his gun bucking. A few minutes ago he'd been pretending there were gunmen on the bluff and now there actually was one! And that hidden gunman up there was after him. Steve had no doubt about it, for lead peppered dangerously close to him. The Ox might have scuttled to safety, but the giant chose to take a hand. Coming to his feet, he hurled himself forward, his great arms upraised, his face twisted. In that moment he was both magnificent and terrible. Three swift steps put his massive body between Steve and that shadow-cloaked killer.

Gun-thunder shook the night. The Ox, reeling, teetered on his toes only to pitch forward on his face, for all the world like a felled oak.

That bullet the Ox had stopped had been intended for Steve. If it had struck him, its impact couldn't have been any more devastating. For the Ox was finished now, drilled through the heart, and those lips that might have named Dawson Reardon's murderer would never speak again.

ten

The Ox was dead. It had all happened so swiftly that even the sight of the giant sprawled upon the ground did not convey the truth to Steve in that first numbing moment. Then, as realization smote him, Steve was charging up the slope with a hoarse cry of rage, heedless of the bullets buzzing about him. Frustration and bitterness goaded him — and grief too, for the Ox, simple creature of instinct, had died defending him.

A few short hours ago, Steve had ridden hell-for-leather out of Battleweed, ridden into the upper valley for the express purpose of capturing the Ox and dragging him to jail for the murder attempt at the rodeo grounds. Since then, he'd come to know that the Ox was his friend — had always been his friend.

On this very spot, fifteen long years before, the Ox had tried to save him when guns had taken their deadly toll. Tonight the Ox had proven his friendship again, sacrificing himself by putting his big body between Steve and the bullets of yonder gunman. All those things, crowding Steve's mind, made him scornful of danger, filling him with a savage desire to close with the hidden killer.

His gun blazing, he carried the fight to the enemy, stampeding up the little hill, zig-zagging as he ran. But on the bluff's crest he paused, panting and breathless, only to find the foe routed. Drumming hoofbeats gave thundering evidence of the manner of the man's escape.

In Battleweed someone had tried to kill Steve from cover. Stumbling in a dark alley, Steve had given up the chase as futile. At the rodeo grounds today, a second sneaking attempt had been made upon his life and that time he'd followed a false trail leading nowhere. Now the killer had struck again — a third time. And this time Steve wasn't going to let him slip through his fingers.

Since the Ox was dead, there was nothing any man could do for the giant except bury him, but that last service would have to wait, for the seconds were precious — each one of them taking the killer further into the night. He *had* to capture the man and that was the spur that drove Steve as relentlessly as his own steel drove his cayuse when, hitting the saddle pony-express style, he wheeled in pursuit.

He had no idea who his quarry might be.

He couldn't even be sure it was the same person who had made all three undercover attempts on his life. It didn't matter. Steve's only enemies in this valley were the Stormes and their hirelings. It had to be one of them who was streaking away into the darkness and he didn't care which one it was. The finish would be the same when Steve laid his hands on him.

But from the first the odds were against Steve in this nocturnal man-hunt. The moon chose to hide its face, scuttling behind banking clouds, and the trail was tangled and treacherous. It wasn't going to be easy to overtake the killer. Branches lashed at Steve, tore at his clothes, almost swept him from the saddle more than once. Fallen trees interlaced the trail at places, hazards for the horse, yet Steve plied quirt and spur as though this were the smooth straightaway of a race track.

But this sort of riding, with no regard for his life or limbs, was very apt to defeat his purpose. It wasn't the sort of race that would go to the swiftest, for if his horse stumbled and broke a leg, there would be no further pursuit. Steve reined short, his ears tuned for sounds to guide him, his horse blowing.

His quarry was still ahead but the

hoofbeats were growing dimmer with distance — proof enough that the killer was lengthening the space between them.

Steve was beginning to realize that his quarry had a tremendous advantage. Rearing Horse Valley was Steve's old home, but he'd been a boy when he'd left here. He remembered the valley fairly well, considering, but his knowledge was bounded by definite landmarks. Back in these tangled foothills were many tangled trails he'd never ridden before — and this was one of them. He had to feel out every inch of the way but the killer was under no such handicap. The edge the man had gained proved it.

It was a maddening situation, doubly so because the urge within him was for speed and more speed. But, resolutely, Steve slowed his pace and headed in the general direction of Battleweed. He was anxious to be out of this wooded country — but when the trail left the timber to become a silver snake writhing across the moon-washed valley floor, there was no rider in sight.

Dismounting, Steve scraped a match aglow and looked for sign. The match burned down to his fingers, flickered out. There was sign enough — too much of it. All of Rearing Horse had headed for Battleweed last morning, following the many trails to town for the rodeo, and the hoofs of a hundred horses had dented this trail in the last twelve hours.

Steve cursed impotently. The killer had eluded him again and he had to face the fact. Still, luck might play into his hands, so Steve headed onward, still riding cautiously instead of swiftly, sparing his horse yet making progress, his ears tuned, his eyes grimly alert. In this manner he came again to Battleweed and with the lights of the town flickering ahead he knew he'd have to chalk up this chase as a failure. Scant chance of finding his unknown quarry in the town — a living needle in a human haystack!

He walked his mount down the dusty street, an angry and disgusted man, and, wrapped in his own thoughts, he was oblivious to all about him until suddenly it struck him that there was something almighty wrong with the town. It was the silence that he felt, more thunderous than exploding guns, an ominous silence, portent of danger, foreboding and chilling.

Yonder was the Buckhorn Saloon. It should be doing a tremendous business tonight. Although many of the rodeo spectators had already headed for home, many others had lingered in Battleweed. Money should be passing both directions over the bar, for the moon-faced bartender would be handing out the betting stakes he'd held.

The winners should be celebrating their good fortune and the losers should be drinking to drown their sorrows and the Buckhorn should be collecting from all of them. True enough, the place blazed with light, the glow of it splashing from its unwashed window to gild the dust of the street. Yet the place was as silent as a tomb.

Where was the clink of glasses — the whir of the roulette wheels — the scraping of bootsoles as cowpokes lined the bar? Where was the medley of boisterous voices, the song of celebrants? It wasn't right, that funeral air that clung to the Buckhorn and to all of Battleweed and Steve was instantly alert for its cause, his hand automatically brushing the gun at his hip.

"Steve!" a voice hissed from the shadows. Steve started, his gun jumping from leather. Wash Winfield was never nearer to death than he was in that instant, for it was he who was hiding there in the darkness. The little bowlegged cowman edged forward, his fingers clamping on Steve's arm as the younger man swung from the saddle.

"What's up?" Steve whispered.

"The Sixty Six-Guns!" Wash spat.

"They've treed the town!"

"Treed the town!"

"They must 'a' got wind that yuh wasn't in town," Wash reported swiftly. "They rode intuh Battleweed half an hour ago, only this time they come in quiet-like instead o' hell fer leather. Maybe some of 'em was already here, mingled with the rodeo crowd."

"Where are they now?" Steve demanded breathlessly.

"They've got things sewed up, I tell yuh. Two or three of them is over at the Buckhorn and they've got the crowd lined up ag'in the bar, sorta keepin' them on ice. They's two or three of 'em wherever men's gathered tonight, keepin' the whole damn town hogtied while Tarn does whatever he's up to. I was standin' near the back door of the Buckhorn and I kept edgin' closer to the door and finally I managed to scoot out just now without 'em seein' me!"

Steve stiffened as he digested this amazing piece of news. The Sixty Six-Guns had struck! Steve hadn't expected they would make a play so soon after their last one had ended disastrously. But they were here — and this time they were playing their cards cautiously, holding the whole town at bay. But that wasn't the thought that was uppermost in Steve's mind. They'd come for Tom Storme! They'd come to rescue Thunder's grandson just as they'd come that other time.

"The jail!" Steve ejaculated. "That's where I'm headin' right now."

Old Wash gave his gunbelt a hitch. "Lead the way," he said.

"No, Wash. You wait here," Steve decided quickly. "Maybe I'll need an ace-in-the-hole and you'll be it. If you want to take a hand, come a-runnin' once you hear gunfire. Got that straight?"

Then Steve was sprinting toward the dark huddle of the jail-building. He'd told Spider Galt to lock up Tom Storme. That meant Tom would be back in his cell again. And Anse Tarn would be there, getting the youngster out of the cell while his hellions made sure that their leader was undisturbed while he was engineering a jail delivery.

But there'd be no jail delivery if Steve Reardon could help it! Hugging the shadows he darted down the deserted street. Deserted? On both boardwalks, pacing in opposite directions, were two bulky figures, a pair of slouching sentries, obviously stationed to keep an eye open for any chance wayfarers who might have escaped the Six-Guns' net. Flattened against a wall, Steve waited until their rounds took them to the farthest point away from the jail. Then he hurried to the building.

On the steps he hesitated cautiously, waiting motionless for a full minute, his ears strained, his nerves tingling. There was no sign of a light but there might be one in the cell corridor. If the connecting door to the marshal's office was closed, such a light wouldn't be visible. Steve thought he heard faint sounds from within but he couldn't be sure for the walls were thick.

Those sentries might be turning back any moment now. With a shrug of his broad shoulders, Steve very carefully put his hand on the doorknob, turned it, pushed the door inward an inch or so. Not a thing happened. Nothing . . . Boldly he flung the door open and stepped inside, closing it behind him. And then something hard was boring into his spine — a gun-barrel.

"Drop yore iron!" a voice grated and Steve let his weapon slip from his fingers to clatter to the floor. There was nothing else he could do.

"Light the lamp, Pokey," the same voice chuckled. "I want to see this jigger's face now that he savvies we was watchin' him from the window all along."

Steve said nothing, for bitterness would

have choked him if he'd tried to speak. Truly he'd blundered into a trap but — worse — he'd failed twice this night — once when he'd tried to capture the man who'd killed the Ox and now again.

He'd been so certain that Anse Tarn, satisfied that his men were doing all the guarding that was necessary, would be devoting himself to other things. But Anse Tarn had been on guard and had bagged himself a prize and there was wolfish satisfaction in his red face as a beard-stubbled gunhawk thumbed a match to life and got the lamp aglow.

"If it ain't the badge-toter!" Tarn grinned and, jerking the Ox's gun from Steve's belt, hurled it into a corner. "Things is a mite different from the last time we met, eh?" His mood changed swiftly, his face twisting with a snarl, and he smashed savagely at Steve with his gun-barrel. The sight ripped a gash on Steve's cheek but he took the punishment silently.

"Got nothin' to say, eh?" Tarn grated, his anger mounting. "Yuh was pretty mouthy last time. I'll —"

A man eased through the connecting doorway from the cell corridor, another beard-stubbled gunhawk who might have been a brother of the one who'd lighted the lamp. "We got Storme's cell unlocked, chief," he reported. "We had to try every damn key in the ring afore we found the right one. We're ready to lope . . ."

Steve scarcely heard him. Standing as though rooted to the floor, his hands aloft, Steve's eyes were busy, measuring the distance between himself and Tarn, gauging that other gunman, scanning the littered desk and the reward dodgers on the wall as though even those things might hold some ghost of a hope.

The window wasn't far away — the window from which Anse Tarn had watched his cautious approach to the jail. This window in the office faced on the street, and it wasn't barred. It was open only an inch, just enough so that the lamp flickered on the desk.

"Fetch Storme along," Tarn ordered. "I got a visitor here, as yuh see, but I'll get rid of him mighty fast. Yuh remember I was supposed to fire once as a signal to the boys so's they could let the town lower its hands while they hit leather. I'll just give 'em the signal but they's no point in wastin' a bullet. Might as well pump it intuh this mouthy gent's carcass!"

Tarn's gun had never wavered from Steve, but now it leveled in Tarn's hand, a slow deliberate gesture patently intended to keep Steve in an agony of suspense until the last moment. And here Steve recognized grim irony. He'd told Wash to come running at the sound of gunfire. Wash would respond when Tarn's gun went off — but Wash would come too late, for a dead man needs no earthly help.

"Here's lead in yore guts!" said Anse Tarn.

And that was when Steve acted. It was futile to make a move, but he had to go down fighting, and there was always the one chance in a hundred that he might save himself. So he lurched, not toward Tarn and his gun, but sidewards, crashing into the desk. The lamp spilled, blotted out into darkness. At the same instant Steve swung his fist, a downward-driven chopping blow that somehow found its mark. His knuckles struck against Tarn's wrist just as the man fired. The bullet thudded into the floor.

Somewhere in the darkness those other two gunmen would be taking cards. But before they could fire, Steve dived head foremost through the window. He landed on all fours outside, glass showering about him, and he rolled blindly as he landed for his sombrero had been smashed down over his eyes. That hat saved his face from being lacerated. Only his hands were bleeding, although his shirt was torn and his skin scraped.

Those things didn't matter. It only mattered that he had to get out of here before Tarn and those others boiled from the jail-building. Steve lurched to his feet and ran into the shadows, ran not with fear goading him but with a blinding anger, And running, he almost collided with Wash Winfield who was legging it toward the jail.

"A gun!" Steve roared. "Give me a gun!"

Wordlessly, Wash thrust a weapon into his hand and Steve, spinning on his heel, was stampeding back toward the jail. But he never had a chance to use that gun. All Battleweed was in turmoil now, released from its spell of silence. The Sixty Six-Guns were piling into saddles everywhere and a group of them had burst from the jail and were heading for horses.

Anse Tarn led them, and it was he who first spied Steve running toward them. Tarn raised his gun, fired once. Something slammed along the side of Steve's head, something that was heavy and hot at the same time. It drained the strength from him, the raking lead that Tarn had loosed, and his knees grew rubbery beneath him and the gun in his hand seemed to weigh a ton.

145

The world was reeling around Steve. He could see the Sixty Six-Guns climbing into saddles and a blurred-looking Tom Storme was being helped into a hull as well. He knew, with his last shred of consciousness, that the Six-Guns had accomplished their purpose and delivered Tom from jail. He could hear, as from a great distance, the triumphant laughter of Anse Tarn. And then Steve's senses deserted him and he pitched face-forward into the dust of the street.

eleven

When Steve opened his aching eyes there was a light almost directly overhead of him and the glare of it seemed so strong that he immediately closed his eyes again. He was weak and dizzy and for several minutes he contented himself by lying quietly, coordinating his thoughts. The brief glimpse of the lamp above him had given him the key to his whereabouts. He was stretched out upon the bar in the Buckhorn Saloon, he realized, and his head was pillowed upon his own sombrero.

He remembered everything then — the trap he'd blundered into in the jail-building, the escape from Anse Tarn, the bullet that had cut him down, that last glimpse of the Sixty Six-Guns escaping with Tom Storme. He became aware that voices were babbling quite near him and he managed to make out coherent words.

"They've gone too damn far this time!" someone was saying, his voice a thin whip of fury. "They can't get away with it! They can't ride in here and take a prisoner outa our jail!"

"Look at the way they tossed lead promiscuous-like once they was ready to leave," another voice cut in, equally angry. "Link Telford's yonder with a bullet-busted arm and Gar Mason was winged and the marshal would be dead if that bullet had been an inch closer, instead of just scrapin' his scalp."

They were all talking at once, their voices blending into a throaty rumble. They were thoroughly aroused, these men of Battleweed, goaded beyond endurance by the latest outrage perpetrated by the Sixty Six-Guns. "They ain't gettin' away with it," one man shouted above the others, his voice shrill with anger. "We gotta ride out to Storme Castle and burn it to the sills. And I'm for doin' it right now!"

It thrilled Steve to listen to them, to know that at long last these small ranchers were ready to challenge the arrogant might of the Stormes. Yet at the same time this wartalk filled him with a certain uneasiness he could neither define nor analyze at the moment.

He opened his eyes again and propped himself upon one elbow. Easing his legs over the edge of the bar, he slid to a standing position. A wave of nausea swept over him, but he fought against it, and Wash Winfield was instantly at his side, steadying him.

"We patched yuh up, Steve, the best we could," the old cowman explained. "Doc Merritt's in the valley, deliverin' a baby. They just creased yuh, Steve; nothin' to worry about. Tarn must 'a' figgered yuh was dead when yuh tumbled. But yuh ain't — and yore turn's comin'. We aim to ride ag'in' them murderin' skunks tonight — the whole batch of 'em — and we aim to have yuh lead us!"

"Wait!" Steve cried, for now he knew why this sort of talk hadn't met with his instant approval. "Maybe that ain't the thing to do! From what I just heard you gents say, it sounded like the Six-Guns scattered some lead before they left. What was the idea of doin' that? Was it just plumb orneriness, or were they deliberately trying to rile us into comin' after them? I'm wondering —"

"Makes no never-mind," one valley rancher boomed. "If it's a fight they crave, we're just the gents to bring one to 'em!"

"And maybe run straight into a trap," Steve argued. "Gents, I'm thinkin' they want us to hit back tonight. And that's just the reason we can't go gallopin' off half-cocked. With the Stormes and their riders and the Sixty Six-Guns throwed in, we'll be buckin' a sizable crowd. There isn't more than a third of us here now. The rest went right home after the rodeo, it looks like, and it would take half the night to round 'em up. I tell you we've got to have our full fighting strength when we tackle the castle! It'd be suicide otherwise!"

"But they snatched Tom Storme from jail," the same rancher countered. "Battleweed's our town and they treed it, then walked into our jail like it was built out of cardboard. We jist can't let 'em get away with that!"

This fellow was angry through and through, so angry that nothing mattered except retaliation against the Stormes and the Six-Guns, and Steve, his glance flicking to other faces in the packed circle that had gathered about him, saw the same grim determination in a dozen faces.

These ranchers were allies of his in a common cause, yet he couldn't endorse this wild plan of theirs, couldn't let them ride into what might prove to be a death trap. There was too much at stake to risk everything on such a mad play. But, at the same time, he couldn't dismiss Tom Storme's escape with a shrug of his shoulders.

No, there was too much involved for that. Rearing Horse ranchers had trembled before the might of the Stormes, deeming them masters here. But Rearing Horse ranchers had found that the Stormes weren't invincible. Hadn't Steve Reardon beat them at the rodeo? Hadn't Steve Reardon thrown Tom Storme in jail and dared the clan to do anything about it? That act had been an omen to many, a sign that the Stormes could be bucked. But the omen would lose its potency if Tom Storme returned safely to his family.

"Gents, most of you know me, I reckon," said Steve, addressing them all. "And you know why I came back to Rearing Horse. You hate the Stormes and so do I — and no man among you hates them more than me. If I wasn't so damn sure the Six-Guns *wanted* us to take their trail, I'd say hit leather, and I'd be proud to be up in front. As it is, we can't risk it till we're better organized. But there's still something that's gotta be done tonight — a one-man job — and I'm gonna do it. As marshal of this town, I'm going to take Tom Storme away from the Sixty Six-Guns. I'm gonna drag him back to jail by the ears — or make a helluva rumpus tryin'!"

He didn't know how they'd react to his proposal. He didn't know whether they'd let him do things his way or whether they'd take matters into their own hands and head recklessly into the valley in spite of his pro-

151

tests. He only knew he had to rule these small ranchers if he was ever to weld them into an organized fighting group capable of striking an effective blow. This was the test.

There was a breathless silence after he made his announcement. Men stared at him, saying nothing, doing nothing, and in that silence a hollow cough was like cannon-ading, a sound to draw every eye to the doorway where a bony man stood just within the batwings, a man in rusty black whose unblinking eyes studied them — Spider Galt.

"Are you loco, Reardon?" Spider Galt asked. "I've heard everything that's been said. If these gents want to ride into the valley and carry the torch and gun to Storme Castle, I say let them do it! It's time for a showdown."

For a moment, Steve could only stare. He wasn't surprised to see Galt here. The man came and went like a shadow, it seemed. But Steve had hardly expected to have Galt opposing him at a time like this.

Steve had seen very little of Jasper Galt since the night when he'd accepted a badge from the man with some misgivings. It had looked as though Galt had given him a free hand in their mutual fight against the Stormes. Certainly Steve had presumed his decisions would be respected in matters like this one, for, by the very nature of their bargain, he was to be the fighting man of the cause — the leader. But now Galt was grasping for the reins of absolute leadership and there was something in his bony face that indicated he would brook no interference. This *was* a showdown, though not exactly the kind Galt meant.

"No, I'm not loco, Galt," Steve said evenly. "I'm just callin' the hand as I see it. Supposin' these boys ride into the valley and get themselves trapped. Supposin' the Stormes got rid of us and then decided to clean out the valley again. Most of the ranchers are home in bed and they're expectin' no trouble, since they don't know anything about what's happened here. Most of 'em would be caught without even a chance to fight back. It'd be hell turned loose — a massacre, far worse than that time years back. We can't risk it."

Galt smiled, arching one Mephistophelian eyebrow. "Too much of what you say is pure guesswork," he observed. "I still say we should be riding — tonight. I'll leave it to the boys here. How about it, gents?"

There he stood, endorsing the very plan that Steve had just vetoed — Jasper Galt, boss of Battleweed, backer of the small ranchers and for that reason a man whose wishes must be respected. A choice had to be made and again there was silence save for the shuffling of bootsoles, the restless movements of hesitant men who eyed each other indecisively. It was a long, endless moment. Then one of the ranchers chose to speak.

"When gents are riled they don't use their heads," he reflected. "Looks to me, though, that Steve Reardon's got this thing figgered out right. Me, I still crave to ride into the upper valley. But if he aims to do it alone, I'm for lettin' him do it his way."

Steve had won. Yet in the moment of his triumph he met the unblinking stare of Spider Galt and knew the alliance between them had ended. Hate was naked in Galt's eyes, a consuming hate all out of proportion to the thing that had prompted it. Steve tore his eyes away. "Wash," he said, low-voiced, "the Ox is dead — out at the Rolling R. I'd consider it kindly if you'd take a couple of the boys and fetch him in."

Turning, Steve strode out of the Buckhorn, the men who had acknowledged his leadership moving aside to make a lane for him. He brushed past Spider Galt without so much as a sideward glance and, out on the street, he went first to the jail-building and fumbled for the gun he'd dropped on the floor. With the weapon in its holster again, he was soon astride a horse and heading out of Battleweed.

The night breeze, whipping against his face, steadied him and made his head cease whirling. He could think clearer now and he began to wonder if he'd chosen wisely. This thing he was about to attempt was loco, crazy — just as foolish, probably, as the thing he'd talked the ranchers out of trying. Lone-handed, he'd bucked the Sixty Six-Guns once before, and luck had played with him that first time. Tonight he'd bucked them again and his luck had been both bad and good — bad because he'd been trapped by Anse Tarn, good because he'd escaped that trap with his life. What sort of luck would he have at the end of this trail?

He didn't know how he was going to pluck Tom Storme from his protectors, but he was going to try. Tom would be heading for the castle, he reasoned. And the Sixty Six-Guns would likely escort the youngster all the way — especially since the wolf pack might be expecting reprisals after deliberately goading the ranchers to the point where the long-suffering little fellows were talking of retaliating.

Something else crowded Steve's mind as he loped along, and that was his break with

Spider Galt. Not that Steve regretted the end of their alliance. Rather, he felt a certain sense of relief, a feeling of freedom that hadn't been truly his since the night he'd bound himself to Galt. But that searing look of hatred Galt had given him . . . ? It puzzled Steve, though he'd felt from the first that Galt had had no real love for him. But why should the man hate him when they were practically strangers to each other in spite of their mutual grudge against the Stormes? Steve shrugged the riddle aside.

Where the trail forked, Steve stopped to look for sign. Here too, there was plenty of sign since both forks had been traveled by ranchers bound for the rodeo. But the Sixty Six-Guns had left the trail and were angling toward the hills. Steve couldn't understand such a move, for Storme Castle lay at the valley's end. Yet there was no doubting that almost three dozen horsemen had been here recently.

They weren't far ahead and by that token Steve realized that he couldn't have been unconscious very long, probably only for the short time it had taken Wash to tote him into the Buckhorn and wrap a crude bandage about his head. Following cautiously, Steve shaped a dozen plans only to discard each scheme as worthless. He was still on the right trail, he knew. Here grass was belly-deep to his horse and Steve wasted no matches looking for sign for it was all too obvious. He threaded through scattered timber, splashed across a narrow creek and found the furrow of trampled grass again.

He was closing in upon the Sixty Six-Guns. In a matter of minutes he saw the dark bulk of the band ahead. Now they were moving across an open, park-like glade. Now the shadows were claiming them, but only briefly, for they spewed forth again to cross another strip of moonlight. A grove of cottonwoods swallowed the group.

Gently nudging his horse, Steve circled wide, moving warily, his eyes on those shadowy trees. The Sixty Six-Guns should be emerging from their concealment, appearing on the farther side. But they didn't. Was this where a trap was being laid? Was this where the little ranchers were to be ambushed if they had the temerity to follow the wolf pack?

Every nerve tingling with an uneasy foreboding, Steve slid from his horse, cautiously lest the creak of saddle leather betray him. Leaving the cayuse ground-anchored, he stooped and darted forward, hugging every shadow and utilizing every bit of cover he could find.

In this manner he reached the grove of trees, a great circle with a gnarled oak in its center, a stricken giant that flung its many arms to trace a weird pattern against the sky. And here he found the Sixty Six-Guns, the whole pack of them. Leaf-filtered moonlight percolated into the thicket to touch the beefy face of Anse Tarn and the others. And Tom Storme was still with them.

Steve had expected him to be.

But Steve hadn't expected to find the youngest of the Stormes sitting his saddle with his hands lashed behind him. He hadn't expected to find the Sixty Six-Guns clustered about Tom with belligerency in their faces while one of that gun-toting group shook out a noose and sent the rope slithering over a low-hanging limb of the oak to dangle above Tom Storme's head.

It didn't make sense to Steve. The intent of the Sixty Six-Guns was all too obvious — but still it was unbelievable, this sight Steve was seeing. But unless he was to doubt the evidence of his own eyes, the Sixty Six-Guns hadn't snatched Tom from jail to return him safely to Storme Castle. The wolf pack was fixing to hang Tom Storme and all the signs said the big youngster would be jerking on the end of a rope in a matter of minutes.

twelve

Sheila had once claimed that Tarn's Sixty Six-Guns were not hirelings of the Storme clan and had also maintained that such was her father's belief. Steve had scoffed at the notion, deeming her opinion to be prejudiced, since the Merritts, admittedly, were friends of the Stormes. The Stormes themselves had denied the allegiance of the gun-crew the day they'd brought the dead gunhand back to Battleweed. Steve had laughed in their faces.

But here was truth — staggering truth. The impending fate of Tom Storme was proof enough that Anse Tarn's crew didn't work for the family. Nor could the Sixty Six-Guns be doing the bidding of Spider Galt, as the Stormes had claimed that same day. Hadn't this gun-crew terrorized the small ranchers, the men who looked upon Galt as their guardian? And hadn't Galt wanted to egg on the small ranchers this very night when the ire of the little fellows had been aroused by the raid of the renegade crew?

The Sixty Six-Guns, then, were playing a hellish lone-wolf game of their own.

Here was mystery and Steve aimed to get to the bottom of it, if he could. But Tom Storme, meanwhile, was doomed, his life span a matter of a few swiftly-marching minutes. There was no reason, of course, why this should be any concern of Steve Reardon's.

Yet Steve was concerned — though, for the life of him, he didn't know why. He only knew that he had a growing impulse to take a hand, but he fought the urge, arguing that even to attempt a rescue would only mean that he would die as well as Tom Storme if he made the try.

Anse Tarn had good reason to hate Steve, for Steve had publicly humiliated him the night when the Sixty Six-Guns had made their first attempt to raid the jail. Tonight Tarn had tried to kill him in Battleweed and Tarn would try again once he learned that Steve was still alive. Why should he, Steve Reardon, rush headlong into danger for the sake of a grandson of Thunder Storme?

Thus it was that Steve, hiding in the shadows and watching the grim preparations for Tom Storme's death-dance, fought the hardest battle of his life. Hate had been Steve's constant saddlemate for many years; a bitter, brooding hatred directed against all who bore the name of

Storme. That hate was warring within him now, but battling against it was something else, something inherent in him — the same sense of tolerance and fair play that had made him fight the clean way when he and Tom Storme had slugged it out, toe to toe, in the Buckhorn Saloon.

Nor could he forget that Tom Storme had fought just as cleanly as he had, both in the saloon and at the rodeo where the battle had been just as personal, and just as bitter. Steve had once told Spider Galt that he, Steve, hadn't goaded Tom into gunplay that first night because Tom, only six years old at the time of Dawson Reardon's death, couldn't possibly have been Steve's sire's murderer. Steve had wanted to humiliate Tom, but he hadn't hankered for the youngster's blood. Should he stand aside now and let it be spilled?

All these things thronged through Steve's mind in less than the space of a minute. Never, so long as he lived, would he be able to call Tom Storme his friend. Spilled blood and searing memories and a lonely grave on the Rolling R would always be a barrier between them. But could he hate Tom as he hated Thunder Storme and Thunder's sons? Steve was honest enough to know he couldn't. That would be like hating the Ox, whose only sin had been a lifetime of faithful service to the Stormes — or hating the sentry who had been true to his salt at the palisade gate.

No, there were varying degrees of hatred, just as there were different kinds of love, and Tom Storme, by the very nature of things, couldn't be in the same category as his range-hogging grandfather, in Steve's mind.

Besides, the Sixty Six-Guns were also Steve's enemies; a ruthless killer-pack who had displayed none of the principle showed by Tom in his manner of fighting. In a sense, any move that Steve made would be a matter of a choice between Anse Tarn and Tom Storme and it required no comparison of the two for Steve to know which was his kind of man. In this manner Steve reached his decision and found himself, ironically enough, an ally of one of the Stormes.

Then he was inching forward through the grass, drawing nearer to the clump of trees. He wished desperately that he'd brought Wash with him, for two men, covering the gun-crew from opposite sides, might be able to keep them at bay. True, Steve had managed to snatch the Ox from the Stormes single-handed simply by throwing a gun on the group and walking off with his prisoner, but there had been light enough then, so he'd been able to keep an eye on all his enemies. This was different. One man wouldn't stand a chance against a group now, since the shadows would be bound to cloak at least one swift-moving, holster-darting hand if some of them risked a play. Steve needed a helper as he'd never needed one before. And suddenly he was aware that he had one.

The grass here was hip-high and a month ago it had been a green and verdant carpet for a green and verdant valley. But the sun that had scorched the rodeo crowd had been beating ceaselessly upon Rearing Horse for more than a month and the grass was yellow and brittle except for those strips that fringed the creeks.

Steve sucked one finger and, testing the breeze with it, smiled wryly to himself. Thumbing a match to life, he cupped it and set the grass afire.

This was a desperate gamble — but it might work! The breeze was blowing toward the creek Steve had crossed, mini-mizing the chances of the fire getting com-pletely out of control and sweeping the valley. It would burn to the creek's bank, and, reaching that natural fire-break, would burn itself out. But before the fire reached the water, the flames would race through that grove of cottonwoods.

Fanning the growing flame with his sombrero, Steve wondered desperately if there was time enough left, for he knew seconds would count. Tom Storme was speaking now, low-voiced, his words inaudible to Steve. But Steve caught a glimpse of Tom's face yonder as the moonlight, filtering through the treetops, touched it and it was eloquent enough, evidence that Tom was at least giving the lynchers a tongue-lashing before they hung him.

The one who held the noose sat his saddle hesitantly but, with an impatient gesture, he raised the rope to drop the noose over Tom's head.

All this Steve saw. Inch by inch the fire had eaten forward while he watched and each inch gave it added momentum. Roaring to throaty life like an unleashed monster, the fire spread out, the blackening grass crackling, the flames, orange-red and lurid, sweeping ahead like a bolting horse beneath the blanket of inky smoke.

"Look yonder!" a gunman suddenly shouted. "Smoke! Can't you smell it? The whole damn valley's afire — and the fire's headin' this way!"

The fire had reached a gulch, shallow as a

spoon but deep enough to suck in the flames like a chimney. Then the fire fanned out, a red dragon with multitudinous tongues engulfing the grove of trees, licking about the trunks, searing the leaves on the lower branches, spreading its own hot brand of havoc. Men were cursing, a note of terror tinging their voices. Horses squealed and bolted. Chaos was laying a smoky hand upon the Sixty Six-Guns, for suddenly they lost all interest in Tom Storme.

Black smoke blotted out the moon, but as that acrid pall swirled, Steve caught one last glimpse of Tom Storme. The big youngster, top-hand horseman that he was, was knee-reining his mount, guiding the animal in a wild lunge out of danger. And no gunman made a move to stop him, for the Sixty Six-Guns, shouting and cursing, were stampeding in sheer panic, motivated by only one desire and that was to get themselves someplace else as quickly as possible.

Tom had eluded his would-be executioners. And in that moment, Steve knew he would never regret his actions in engineering Tom's escape. A man had to live with himself. If there would be remorse for a man who stood by and watched a cold-blooded killing take place, Steve would never know such remorse. He had played this hand as his conscience had dictated. And he wasn't sorry.

A dead cottonwood ignited and became a gigantic torch that made daylight out of darkness, painting the night sky a scarlet hue, sending sparks showering upward. Steve darted across the blackened swath of ground where the fire had been, seeking the cover of the shadows as he ran. He'd left his horse between the cottonwoods and the creek before he'd maneuvered around to get the breeze to his back. Without a doubt his horse had already bolted. Steve was afoot, the greatest curse that can befall a cowboy, but he meant to remedy that handicap just as quickly as possible. Opportunity played into his hands sooner than he expected.

Out of the fire's circle of light and beyond that blasting, searing heat, he was heading toward the creek, angling along a brushy slope as he went. Just behind him something thrashed among the bushes, for all the world like a rampaging grizzly. It was one of the Sixty Six-Guns.

The fellow had given his terror-stricken horse its head but the mount had exhausted itself by bolting up the slope. Now it floundered along, heaving and blowing, while the rider pawed at his smoke-filled, streaming eyes. That much Steve saw. Then he was launching himself upon the gunman, dragging him from the saddle.

Steve wanted that horse. Since the group of gunhands had taken a dozen different directions in their wild rout, Steve was gambling that none of the others would be close enough to side this particular gun-hog before Steve could subdue him. The man, scrawny and flat-chested, a weasel-faced sort of a killer, was no match for Steve. Steve had the gunman under him almost instantly and though the man squirmed, kicking and clawing in blind terror, Steve soon had him spread-eagled upon the ground. The fellow, staring, gasped in astonishment as he recognized his assailant.

"Reardon! Anse claimed he left yuh kickin' in the dust back in Battleweed — a gone gander. It was you started that fire. You must 'a' did it to save Tom Storme. Gawd, we never figgered yuh'd lift a hand to help out one of the Storme family . . ."

Steve didn't mean to waste time bandying useless words with the man. That wasn't his purpose at the moment. But now, with this man at his mercy, Steve's mind harked back to the mystery that had manifested itself in the cottonwoods — the mystery behind the purpose of the Sixty Six-Guns. Listening intently, Steve heard only the crackle and roar of the grass fire as it raced below them, a muted roar now for the fire had almost burned itself out. They were alone.

"Why were you going to hang Tom Storme?" Steve demanded. "What was the idea of that?"

"The chief told us to," the gunman spluttered. "Shucks, I shore didn't figger yuh give a damn about any of the Stormes. The chief told us tuh snake Tom outa jail and then take him intuh the valley and beef him. It was Anse Tarn's idea to hang him, 'stead of puttin' a bullet in him and gettin' it over with quick. Anse, he's shore one gent that enjoys seein' an air-dance."

"The chief?" Steve repeated. "You mean there's somebody that's higher up, a gent who gives Tarn his orders? You mean you've hired out your guns to somebody hereabouts, somebody who's against both the Stormes and the small ranchers. Who is it?"

The gunman chose to be sullen. "I ain't sayin'," he countered stubbornly.

Steve's hands were pinioning the spread-eagled gunman's arms to the ground. Steve moved himself forward, shifting his weight and placing his knees upon his prisoner's stringy biceps. With his hands free, Steve wrapped his fingers around the fellow's neck and squeezed, none too gently.

"Talk!" Steve hissed. "You ever see a rooster get its neck wrung plumb off? I crave to know who hired you skunks to come to Rearing Horse and do your deviltry. Just why have you been raisin' hell in general with the small ranchers, and tryin' to bang Stormes on the side? Talk up — or I'll wring your scrawny head off and feed it to the coyotes!"

It was cold-blooded, that threat; the sort of threat to thoroughly scare this cold-blooded killer. The fellow choked.

"Don't!" he begged. "I ain't lettin' myself get killed just to keep a secret that everybody in the valley's gonna know when the cards are faced — which is likely to be pronto. Spider Galt's the paymaster for my bunch — the gent that gives the orders!"

Limbs were snapping in the cottonwood which was still blazing, not a hundred yards away — noise enough to make Steve believe he hadn't heard right. "Galt!" he echoed and his fingers tightened on the gunman's throat again: "You're lying! Galt's been lending money to the little fellers — money to build new barns to replace the ones you snakes burned — money to buy lead to fight you. Galt's maybe a cagey gent who watches out for himself pretty close, but it just don't make sense that he'd be hirin' you gents for the kind of work you've been doin'. Talk up

— and talk straight this time!"

"Stop and figger," the gunman managed to gasp, for Steve had almost shut off his wind. "Galt's loaned money to the little fellers and them gents has mortgaged their spreads to Galt to get the *dinero*. Likewise them ranchers has been blamin' things onto the Stormes — things *we* did. Supposin' them little fellers get proddy enough to up and drive the Stormes outa the valley? Ever hear of a gent playin' both ends all in the middle? Galt's already got the little fellers where he wants 'em. With the Stormes gone, Galt'd own Rearing Hoss. Can't yuh savvy his game?"

Steve could savvy. At first the pattern of it was slow in shaping but with the pieces falling into place, one by one, he could see it all — and it wasn't exactly a pretty picture.

He'd mistrusted Galt at first sight, guessing that the man was unscrupulous and self-centered. But Galt had hated the Stormes, and in that respect Steve had found a common cause with the man. He'd lined up with Galt, but he'd made a blindman's bargain, for he'd been a pawn in Jasper Galt's game. Small wonder that Galt had been trying to urge the ranchers to attack Storme Castle tonight! With one faction spending its strength in a death struggle against the other, Galt's grip on the valley would have been that much stronger!

"Spider Galt!" Steve said slowly. "He was spinning a pretty tight web."

"And it's caught one fly, it looks like," a voice said, so close that it might have been at Steve's elbow. Instantly Steve was upon his feet, his hand dropping toward his gun. But his fingers froze halfway to his holster for he was reaching too late.

With the crackle of the dying fire to blanket any sound they might have made, a half-dozen men had managed to be almost upon Steve without his having any inkling of their nearness. Now the group stood watching him coldly, leveled guns in their fists. Anse Tarn was one of the bunch, his eyebrows singed away, his beefy face aglow with a savage satisfaction. The others belonged to Tarn's pack — a smoke begrimed handful of men. But there was one in the group who must have just joined it. He was the one who had spoken.

"Spider Galt!" Steve gasped.

"I've been right behind you almost since the moment you left Battleweed," the lanky black-clad man said sardonically. "Seems like I came along too late to be in on most of the excitement. But maybe —"

"Just a minute, chief," Anse Tarn interjected. "This jigger seems to take a helluva lot of killin' — but that's O.K. with me, seein' as how he could die twenty times and it wouldn't be enough to suit me. They's somethin' I took a whack at doin' back in Battleweed, but we was kinda in a hurry that time and I botched it. This time I can maybe do a better job . . ."

He gestured and two of his men, leaping forward, grasped Steve's arms. One of them plucked Steve's gun from its holster, hurled the weapon into the darkness. Steve submitted, for there was no choice. He only began to struggle when he understood the intent of Anse Tarn — and then it was too late.

Smiling crookedly, Anse Tarn came forward, his arm raised. He swung his gun-barrel downward in a vicious, chopping blow. Steve, twisting his head aside, managed to save himself from a split skull and Wash Winfield's makeshift bandage was some slight protection too. But the gun-barrel grazed the side of his head, the wounded side, and a million lights danced before his eyes. The grinning face of Anse Tarn seemed to fade before him. Then Steve's senses deserted him and for the second time that night he tumbled into bottomless darkness . . .

thirteen

It was morning when Steve opened his smarting eyes and at first he failed to recognize his surroundings. He was only conscious that he lay stretched upon a hard bed or cot of some sort, but his whereabouts escaped him in the blurred confusion of awakening.

His head throbbed, and because he wondered why, he began to remember the events that had preceded unconsciousness. His fingers strayed to his head. His bandage was gone, but it was no longer needed, for the blood had clotted. He was alive — a miracle in itself. He managed to prop himself upon his elbows and simultaneously became aware of three things, each of them significant.

He was fully clothed, even to boots and spurs, but his guns were gone and so was the badge he'd worn on his shirt. It had been ripped away. And since the morning sun, streaming through a window, laid a striped pattern across him, he jerked his eyes from wall to wall in startled understanding. This was Battleweed's jail and he was in one of the cells — the very cell that Tom Storme had occupied!

From the cot he could see the barred front of the cell, facing upon the corridor, and he could see into the corridor as well. He made his third discovery then. Beyond the bars waited Jasper Galt. His bony frame folded into a sort of inverted N, the man squatted upon a three-legged stool; silent, impassive, his shrewd unblinking eyes upon Steve in alert expectation as though he'd seen the signs of Steve's return to consciousness and had posted himself here in anticipation of Steve's rude awakening.

"So you've come around, eh?" Galt observed with apparent satisfaction. "And you're surprised to find yourself in jail. It will interest you, no doubt, to learn that you're being held here charged with murdering the Ox out at the old Rolling R last night."

"Murderin' the Ox," Steve repeated weakly and then the import of it, striking him like a body blow, gave him the strength of anger. "Murderin' the Ox!" he repeated. "What do you mean? What sort of frame-up is this, Galt? Why, damn you — !"

Dropping his legs to the floor, Steve came to his feet wrathfully. It was more than Galt's accusation that was goading him, for he was remembering Galt's perfidy and the proof of it that had come when Galt had admitted his amazing alliance with the Sixty Six-Guns by appearing with the gun-crew last night. But Steve had overestimated his strength.

He took three tottering steps toward the bars before he realized how senseless and futile his action was. He didn't have strength enough to tear away paper bars, much less steel ones. Yet fear flamed in Galt's eyes and the man dipped a bony hand beneath his rusty black coat where Steve saw the significant bulge of a shoulder holster. Steve sank limply upon the cot's edge.

"You were all set to pull the jail to pieces," Galt said mockingly. "Now I don't think the new marshal would have liked that. But I've forgotten. You're not up-to-date on events hereabouts, are you? Anse Tarn is town marshal now. I appointed him last night. He's highly qualified, too. Rather impetuous, but most of the time he does things as he's told to do them. I didn't intend for him to try and cave in your head last night. But Anse just naturally hates your guts so bad that he forgot himself."

Steve looked at him in amazement. "You've made Tarn marshal!" he gasped. "Then you're tippin' your hand, lettin' everybody know that the Sixty Six-Guns ride for you instead of the Stormes. Do you think the little fellers, hatin' the Six-Guns like they do, will let you get away with this, Galt? You've cut your own throat this time!"

Galt laughed. "Think so?" he asked. "The little fellers proved last night that it was you they were going to follow, not me. But what do I care about those two-bit cownurses! They never had ten-cents' worth of guts between the bunch of 'em and they've only started gettin' proddy since you showed up to point the way."

He paused, running his bony fingers through his thin hair. "Last night the Six-Guns treed Battleweed and made the whole damn town dance to their tune," he went on. "Now they've taken over the town again and whatever they do is legal, since they're all deputies of Anse Tarn. Anse is getting a whale of a kick out of running around with a badge on his vest and he'll get a bigger kick out of hanging you for killing the Ox. And I'm thinkin' all of the fight will go out of the little fellers in a hurry when they see their brave leader dangling from a gallows!"

Steve's head still ached, but it was clearing a little and he could think coherently now. That was why he felt the thrust of a swift suspicion.

"So you're chargin' me with killing the Ox," he observed. "Yet I only told Wash Winfield about what happened. That was last night when I asked him to go and fetch the body in. You were in the Buckhorn at the time but you didn't hear me and you followed me into the valley right afterwards. How did *you* know the Ox was dead?"

Galt arched his Mephistophelian eyebrows and smiled. "Shucks, maybe I also followed you into the valley the first time you went, the time you trailed the Stormes after the rodeo, for all you know. It didn't take long to lock up Tom Storme. You see, I get around more than folks think. Why, I might have even cut ahead of you and been hidin' that night somebody turned lead loose on you here in Battleweed. Remember?"

Steve, remembering all too well, narrowed his eyes, his fingers straying instinctively to his wounded shoulder.

"And perhaps I had a hand in fixing Angelmaker's saddle," Galt went on in obvious enjoyment. "A gent is sometimes more under cover in a crowd than when he thinks he's alone. And it was no trick to make sure that you were the one who'd draw Angelmaker."

"You couldn't have worked that!" Steve blurted. "Not unless Cow Rowley was in cahoots with you. And from the way he talked when your name came up, he didn't have any more use for you than he had for a sidewinder!"

"So?" Galt grinned. "Remember, the judge only had half-a-dozen slips left in his sombrero and the old gent was too wrapped up in Tom Storme's last ride to be watching anything else. Supposing somebody snatched those slips, put in six other slips, *all* of them having Angelmaker's name. Stands to reason you were bound to draw Angelmaker when you picked a slip. Likewise it stands to reason that nobody ever saw through the change, since you made the last ride and nobody drew another slip."

Steve understood all too well. This was equivalent to a confession that Galt himself had made all three undercover attempts to murder him. Galt, then, had killed the Ox while trying to kill Steve.

But why? That was the thing Steve couldn't savvy. Why had Galt tried so hard to kill him when their trails had never crossed before Steve's return to Battleweed? Galt might have reason now to kill him, since the small ranchers had swerved their allegiance from Galt to Steve. But Galt had

had no such motive that first night.

Lifting his eyes, he searched Galt's sardonic face, seeing the gloating light in the bony man's eyes. The man was mad! That was the only answer there could be, yet Steve wasn't satisfied with his own solution. If Galt were mad, there was deliberate method to much of his madness.

"I'm beginning to savvy," Steve said slowly. "That gunhog I bulldogged last night was tellin' it straight — all of it. It was you that brought in the Sixty Six-Guns, just like he said, as part of a scheme to get control of the valley. Is that it?"

Galt chuckled. "The railroad's coming through here. I told you that before. They'll want right of way down Rearing House and they'll pay plenty to get it. And they'll pay me! I'll be master here, savvy. Everything has worked my way. First I figured on riling the small ranchers, getting them to drive out the Stormes. The Sixty Six-Guns helped by givin' the little fellers hell and making them think the Stormes was behind it all, but the ranchers never got to the fighting point. The name of Thunder Storme kept them paralyzed. But meantime the little fellows borrowed money from me and mortgaged their spreads for security. This end of the valley is practically mine."

"And the Stormes — ?" Steve probed.

"I'd hoped the little fellows would get proddy and drive out the Stormes and then the upper valley would be mine for the taking. They might have tried it last night, but you horned in and talked them out of it. Now I can't wait for them to strike, so I'm playin' my cards different . . ."

"So it seems," Steve remarked drily.

"The railroad is laying steel fast, getting too near the valley. The stage, last night, brought a letter to my land-office, a letter inquiring about ownerships in the valley. Officials will probably be here to dicker for right of way within a week. Before that time the Sixty Six-Guns will strike at the Stormes — and they'll strike hard! That's why I wanted them to beef Tom Storme last night after I told them where they'd find the keys to get Tom out of this cell. It meant one less gun against us at showdown. But Tom Storme got clear away, thanks to your meddling. But it makes no never mind, for we'll wipe them out anyway . . .

"You'd like to see that part of it, wouldn't you, Reardon? You'd like to see Storme Castle going up in smoke. But you won't be living then. When one man hates another as much as I hate you, the itch of his trigger finger drives him crazy!"

"You hate — you've hated me from the first!" Steve said. "In the name of common sense, Galt — why?"

"Because you're the living image of Dawson Reardon and I hated him! You never knew that, eh? I wasn't sure at first. But listen — Dawson Reardon took the one thing in this world that I ever wanted and didn't get. They call me Spider Galt. Maybe it isn't a flattering name. But when I spin my webs they always bring me whatever I crave. They failed me only once. There was a girl — a beautiful girl. When she looked at me there was something in her eyes — something you see in the eyes of any woman when a toad hops across her path. But she didn't look at Dawson Reardon that way. She married him — *him*, a little two-bit rancher! She chose him instead of me! Now can you savvy why I hate the very sight of you?"

"God!" Steve whispered.

"I've never hated any man so much as I hated Daw Reardon. I'd have killed him. But Thunder Storme beat me to it. Yes, it was old Thunder himself who squeezed the trigger. Giving the devil his dues, it probably wasn't Thunder's way to shoot a man in the back but he didn't have much choice. The Stormes had ringed the Rolling R and

Daw Reardon charged up the bluff, his guns spouting. Nathan Storme was up there alone and wounded and Thunder was behind your father so Thunder cut him down. I could have told you that the first night you were in Battleweed.

"I kept silent. If I'd told you the truth, you'd have burned leather to Storme Castle to hunt down Thunder. You'd have busted your way right to Thunder's throne and they'd have cut you down like a trapped coyote. *I* wanted to do the trigger squeezing on that chore!"

"So you were out to kill me from the first!" Steve murmured in awed understanding.

"From the first! You'll never know how near to death you were that night you sat across my desk from me in my office. There was a gun in the drawer, not six inches away. But when I asked you how gun-handy you were, asked you why you hadn't burned down Tom Storme, you told me it wasn't gun-swift you were lacking. I couldn't take the chance then, so I waited till after you left.

"At first the only thing that mattered was to see you kicking in the dust. But this way is better. That's why I fetched you here and gave you time to recover consciousness — to tell you the truth, to watch your face, to see you squirm before you died. I made you marshal. That tickled me, to keep you where I wanted you, to use you as my tool against the Stormes. Now I've got things the way I want them. I don't need you any more, you poor, blind fool!"

He gasped, spent by his own passion, and Steve was weak too, not so much from his wounds as from the horror that had swept him as he'd listened to the mouthings of this bitter, hate-filled man. Then Galt, his eyes agleam again, abruptly changed the subject.

"She died bringing you into this world," he hissed. "I hate you for that, too. She was married to Daw Reardon, but so long as she was alive, I'd never have quit trying to get her. I would have won in the end — I always win. But she died and all I ever had of her was *this*. And I had to steal it from the Rolling R . . ."

He dipped into a coat pocket with his left hand and fished out a small golden locket. He caressed it after a fashion, rubbing one long thumb over it. Then, snapping it open, he extended it between the cell bars.

Steve came to his feet almost reverently. He'd never known the mother who'd died giving him birth and, so far as he could re-member, he'd never seen a picture of her. His steps were stronger as he crossed the cell this time and Spider Galt, watching him intently and seeing the signs of his returning strength, drew a six-gun with his right hand, cocked it and kept it leveled.

Steve was staring at the open locket. Once it had held two pictures and the other one had probably been of Dawson Reardon. But the other picture had been viciously removed with a pen-knife; its jagged edges still clinging to the frame. That was undoubtedly Jasper Galt's work and was understandable enough. The second picture was intact.

And with his eyes upon that picture, Steve felt his senses reeling and it wasn't his wounds of the night before that made his head swim. His mother! Cameo-faced, she was beautiful in a classic sort of way, a beauty that was spiritual as well as physical. But it wasn't the perfection of face and feature, nor the character of the woman, giving life to this dull, lusterless tintype, that astonished Steve.

If his mother's hair had been gray instead of golden, and if the years had had time to etch lines about her mouth and forehead, she would have been Steve's "ghost lady," that phantom woman of the night whom Steve had long considered as only the figment of a feverish boy's imagination.

fourteen

While Steve was standing there as though rooted to the floor, his eyes wide, his jaw sagging, the door to the marshal's office slammed open, slammed shut, and Anse Tarn, badge and all, stampeded into the cell corridor. His red face was redder than ever, flushed with excitement.

"Boss!" he shouted. "They's hell to pay! Yuh overplayed yore hand this time! With me wearin' this badge, the whole damn town knows I'm yore huckleberry. Yuh know them small ranchers hate me and my bunch — and they hate us a heap worse after last night. Yuh'd 'a' done better to keep 'em thinkin' we was sidin' the Stormes until showdown."

"What are you driving at?" Galt demanded truculently.

"A bunch of the little fellers just drifted into town and they've got the lay o' the land," Tarn spluttered. "They're over to the Buckhorn, a-grumblin' and a-sayin' that yuh played 'em for fools. If they find out we've got Reardon in here, things is liable to bust wide open! They've got him pegged for a little tin god with purty red wheels . . ."

Snatching the locket from beneath Steve's fascinated eyes, Spider Galt came to his feet so quickly as to overturn the stool.

"Come on!" he shouted. "We'll go over there and let those cow-nurses see the sight of a few shooting irons. Those little fellows have always done a heap of talking but they haven't got the guts of a gopher. They were full of fire last night, but I'm bettin' that's all burned out by now. So long as there's just a few of them grumbling, we've nothing much to worry about."

His rusty black coat flapping behind him, Galt strode out of the corridor and into the office, Anse Tarn at his heels, the gunhog pausing long enough to stare malevolently at Steve. Then the outer door slammed again and Steve was alone.

Alone? A thousand puzzling questions kept him company, thronging through his mind, making his head spin.

He'd learned things from Spider Galt — things that lifted the veil from one mystery only to present the shadowy face of another. He'd learned the name of Dawson Reardon's murderer! He'd gained that much after being cheated out of the truth by the untimely death of the Ox. He'd gotten the deadwood on old Thunder at long last.

But Thunder Storme was safe and secure in Storme Castle while Steve was locked in Battleweed's jail, a helpless fly in the web of Spider Galt who hated him as much as Steve hated the Stormes.

It was agony, more excruciating than any physical pain, to know what Steve now knew and to be unable to do a single thing about it. Crossing to the door again, Steve gripped the bars to shake them in impotent fury, realizing full well that the very action was childish and foolish. But as he touched the door a thrill shot through him for the door gave, its unoiled hinges protesting. With startled eyes, Steve watched the door swing open.

This was amazing — so amazing that it filled Steve with a vague alarm. For a long moment he stood hesitantly, held by a hunch that the situation was decidedly not as it should be. Cell doors were not things that were carelessly left unlocked.

Stepping very cautiously into the corridor where a quick glance proved that the other cells were empty, he peered into the marshal's office, adjacent to the cell row, and found it empty too.

There was no one in the building but himself and that, at least, was reassuring. His bootheels clicking against the floor, he crossed to the littered desk, kerosene soaked and strewed with the wreckage of the lamp he'd upset when he'd escaped Anse Tarn's death-trap the night before. He was hoping against hope that he'd find a gun somewhere. But the desk drawers, crammed with a hundred odds and ends, contained no weapon of any sort.

Steve paused, gnawing at his under lip, running his fingers through his blood-clotted hair. Wary as a beast who scents a trap, he stood in the office looking through the broken window upon the sun-splashed street. Yonderly was Hop Gow's restaurant, flies droning around the doorway, buzzing about slant-eyed old Hop Gow himself who stood there, his wrinkled hands tucked into his voluminous sleeves, his parchment-like face as impassive as the peaks. In the dusty street a dog stretched in drowsy contentment, dreaming, perhaps, of a range where all the jackrabbits were hobbled. Here was peace and the pathway to freedom.

Turning on his heel, Steve left the office to pace down the corridor to the building's rear door. It was fastened on the inside by a slip-bolt and Steve carefully opened the door and peered into the narrow, debris-littered alleyway beyond. Nobody was in sight. Slowly, thoughtfully, Steve closed the door and returned to the office.

Had Spider Galt made a slip? Had the unlocked cell door been an oversight which Galt was likely to be regretting shortly? Steve wanted to think so.

Yet Spider Galt, prompted by a desire to see his victim squirm, had bared all his plans and confessed the full extent of his deviltry, told secrets to Steve that only a grave could hold inviolate. It didn't make sense that Galt would have overlooked any precautions after that. And Spider Galt, Steve remembered, had reached for his gun when Steve had first lunged toward the cell door, even though bars had separated the pair of them. That was queer. Had Galt *known* all along that the door was unlocked?

Steve didn't know. Yet it didn't suit him to stand here in futile meditation for this very inaction made him just as much a prisoner as though he were locked in the cell. Tarn and Galt would return shortly and if that unlocked door had been an oversight, they'd make mighty sure that it was locked after they herded him back into the cell.

If, on the other hand, this were all some sort of trap purposely baited by Spider Galt, then the only way to test the trap was to step into it!

Squaring his broad shoulders without

being conscious of the gesture, Steve made a choice. He could leave by either door and if this weren't a trap, it didn't make any difference which door he used. But if it were a trap, the back door would be the most dangerous, probably, because it *appeared* to be the safest. He took a step toward the front door. Then he was pivoting on his heel, crouching, his hand automatically slapping against his gunless thigh.

A sound had reached him. The door at the end of the cell corridor was opening. Who was it? Anse Tarn? Spider Galt? One of the Sixty Six-Guns?

But it was Sheila, her face flushed with excitement, who darted inside. "Come, Steve — this way!" she cried breathlessly, her voice low. "Come quickly! There's no time now for talking."

He was halfway down the corridor to meet her and she grasped his hand, almost dragging him through the rear doorway. Then they were out of the building and side by side they sped down the alleyway in silence, Sheila tugging at his hand as though the devil were at their heels. Ernie Ide's livery stable was on this side of the street and they bobbed through the rear doorway of the place and into the stable's shadowy depths and there Sheila stood panting.

"We're safe — for the time being," she gasped. "They'll have men in the alleyway in another few minutes. I just heard their plans by accident. I was in Grover's Mercantile doing some shopping and two of those gunmen were standing on the porch talking. The town's full of them, you know. They plan on ringing the jail with men — shooting you down as you ventured out."

Now the mystery of the unlocked cell was no longer a mystery for Steve understood all too well. *Ley de Fuga!* Down along the Rio Grande, Steve had heard of the Mexican law of escape, the grim law that made a jail-breaking fugitive a fair target for anybody's gun. Sometimes a political prisoner who had been jailed with very little evidence against him, found the door to escape open only to learn, too late, that he was walking, not to freedom, but to death. *"Ley de Fuga,"* some unofficial executioner would say with a wink, and the matter was closed — forever.

Jasper Galt had planned to apply the same idea in Montana. Yet Steve sensed that there was more behind this plan than a scheme to legalize a murder. Spider Galt was the law in Battleweed and Galt, with the Sixty Six-Guns to back him, didn't have to be concerned with appearances when he made a killing.

No, Spider Galt had wanted to play a cat-and-mouse game, to dangle the hope of freedom before Steve's eager eyes, to make Steve believe that luck was playing his way, and then to shoot him down just when Steve thought freedom was within reach.

"Sheila," Steve said huskily. "I would have walked right into it. I was going to step outside the front door when you showed up. You just saved my life . . ."

He hadn't seen her to talk to her since the day when they'd stood beside Angelmaker's corral and the Stormes had ridden into Battleweed to return the body of the dead gunman. She'd been angry with him then, berating him for the hatred he bore the Stormes. She'd left him after giving him a tongue-lashing. But she wasn't angry now. Concern was in her eyes and her lips were trembling and she looked very small and very scared — and very appealing.

A dozen saddle horses stomped in as many stalls, but old Ernie Ide, the hostler, was gone somewhere and the man and the girl were alone. It wasn't a place for romance to flower, this livery stable. Yet something in Sheila's eyes, lifted to his, made Steve heedless of the time and place and suddenly his arms were around her and the danger he'd just escaped seemed a distant, shadowy, unimportant thing, for his lips were pressed to hers. It was a long kiss, chaste yet passionate, heart-given and heart-taken. But Sheila tore herself from Steve's arms, her face flaming.

"I hate you!" she cried. "I hate you! I know why you did that! You've heard that Tom Storme likes me. You've heard that maybe one of these days he'll ask me to marry him. It's just some more of your revenge — another way of beating Tom Storme!"

Steve, speechless before her wrath, could only grasp her trembling shoulders until he found words.

"Sheila," he said sincerely, "maybe I've got this coming to me — considerin' things I've said and things I've done. But if I've stacked so low in your eyes that you believe what you just said about me — then I'm plumb sorry. But believe me — I don't fight women, and I don't use women in my fight. Does Tom mean so much to you?"

"He's a friend, nothing more," she said. "I like him and I respect him. There are many things about him worth respecting — things you could see if your hate wasn't blinding you. I'm — I'm sorry, Steve, for what I insinuated. It was just that I was so afraid that — that you didn't mean it. It —

it's so important and has been, I think, ever since those schooldays so long, long ago . . ."

It was as much as any man could ever want to hear, but reality reared itself, an obnoxious shadow across Steve's thoughts. "Look," he said swiftly. "There isn't time for talking here, either. They'll find the jail empty and they'll hunt me down. I can't risk that now — especially with you here. And I've got to get out of here and get to Storme Castle. But when I come back, dear, we'll be taking up where we just left off!"

"Storme Castle! You've learned something. I can see it in your face. You're going there for a showdown! Oh, Steve . . . !"

"But I've got to," Steve insisted. "Yes, I know you and your father can't see it my way. I know your father hinted at some dark secret that would make me sorry. But can't you see, dear? It's more important than ever, now, that I bring this business to a finish. I'm not a free man, Sheila — not while this thing is hanging over me. I had no right to kiss you. I can't even let myself think about you. Not for a while. That's why I've got to bring this affair to its finish — so I can call my soul my own — so I can come back — to you."

She nodded numbly. "Maybe I've been

wrong," she conceded. "Maybe father has been wrong, too. I don't know what he hinted at. Honestly I don't. It must be some kind of professional secret he couldn't tell even me. But go, Steve — if that's what your heart tells you to do."

"You — you do understand, then?" he asked.

"I'm trying to," she said. "If the only thing that will take the hate out of you is to have it burned out, that's the way it will have to be, I guess. I can't stop you, Steve. I've tried to use my head instead of my heart, but it's no use. Whatever is your fight, has to be my fight too, Steve. When you come back — I'll be waiting . . ."

He kissed her again and her surrender was wholehearted this time. She clung to him for a breathless moment and there was no heart in him to let her go. He was a man whose pattern of life had been shaped by hatred and now he'd found love. Ironically, he had to fulfil his obligation to the first master before he could acknowledge the second. Reluctantly, he tore himself away.

Running his eyes over the horses in the stalls, he selected a fiddle-footed sorrel, built for speed and stamina. Tossing gear onto the horse, Steve talked as he worked. All Battleweed knew of Galt's alliance with the Sixty Six-Guns, of course, but Steve told Sheila the rest of it, sketching Galt's plan to dominate the valley.

"I played right into his hands," Steve confessed ruefully. "He's against the Stormes too, and that's the only thing that made me have anything to do with him from the first. But my fight and his fight are two different things. I'm lone-wolfin' it from here on out. It'll be me against both packs of 'em."

There were other things he might have spoken of — Spider Galt's hatred for him and his father before him — the mysterious resemblance of his mother to the "ghost lady" — the empty coffin that had been buried out at the Rolling R. But there wasn't time for that. A new idea was forming in Steve's head, and even after the sorrel was saddled, there were things to do.

Rummaging in a saddlebag, Steve found a loaded six-gun and a handful of cartridges which he pocketed. There was also a pair of field-glasses and he took these after a moment's reflection. But his real interest was in ropes, and he selected a dozen lariats from wall pegs, examined them briefly to see that they were in good condition, then fastened them to the saddle of the mount he'd chosen. Then he climbed up into the hull.

He chose to go out the front way. The alley behind dead-ended and, besides, Steve had a hunch that a wild, unexpected dash might have its merits. The Sity Six-Guns, still expecting him to emerge from the jail, would be unprepared for his appearance at any other point. Flourishing the gun in a last farewell to Sheila, he sank steel into the sorrel.

Then he was out into the street, a sun-washed gauntlet where death lay waiting. But death chose to slumber at first. Steve flashed past Hop Gow's, roweled past the jail-building, the dust boiling behind him, the sleepy dog, no longer sleepy, *ki-yi*-ing to the shelter of a porch. Someone shouted in amazement and the shout was echoed from the far side of the street as the startled gunmen, posted at advantageous points, found their quarry a-horse and in flight.

It was a signal for all hell to let loose. The thunder of a dozen guns blended to echo from the false fronts, a crashing refrain that multiplied itself. Bullets buzzed about Steve but he was moving too swiftly to make a good target and his own gun was speaking now.

Lead plucked at his sleeve, fanned his cheek. Lead kicked at the dust, goading the sorrel to a frenzy of speed. Men were boiling out of the Buckhorn and leading them was Spider Galt. Steve had a glimpse of the man whose bony face was livid with rage. He snapped a shot toward Galt, knowing, even as the gun bucked, that he'd aimed too hastily and had missed. Then Steve was at the end of the street and beyond the gauntlet.

But was he? Here an unused building, decrepit and unpainted, flanked him, a two-story affair. In an upper window a bearded gunman eyed Steve over the barrel of a belching rifle. The fellow could shoot and his bullets were peppering about Steve, entirely too close for comfort.

Steve fired — once, twice. The gunman jerked upward like some grotesque jack-in-a-box, doubled, and slumped over the window sill. He seemed to hang there for an eternity, then slowly, ever so slowly, his bulky body slipped forward and began to somersault downward. Nauseated, Steve dragged his eyes away.

His gun was empty and he punched fresh cartridges into it as he rode, loading from his pocket. But now the danger was minimized, for he was clear of the town and thundering up the valley. Guns still barked behind him, but the distance was too great for effective shooting. And Steve wasn't overly worried about pursuit. This horse beneath him had been reared to run, and by the time the disgruntled gun-crew was into saddles, Steve would have the edge on them that would spell escape.

He'd slipped unscathed through the closing jaws of Spider Galt's gun-trap, but there was little consolation in that when he reflected that he was very likely hopping from the frying pan into the fire. He was heading for Storme Castle — and a showdown with old Thunder himself. There would be guns to greet him at the end of this trail — guns as hungry for his hide as those he'd just put behind him.

fifteen

It was the sort of day to make a man look forward to living, rather than dying.

The dry spell that had gripped Rearing Horse had been broken, at least in the upper valley, by a bit of rain which must have come while Steve lay unconscious the night before. Now there was a sparkle to the grass as though a fairy's wand had jeweled it; a sweet, clean freshness to the air that gave it an intoxicating tang. The Bitter Roots, those mountains of many moods, chose to be mysterious and sullen this morning, wrapping their rocky crests in foggy veils, grayish wisps known as "squaws," and scowling upon the valley below.

But Steve, thundering into Rearing Horse Valley once again, had his eyes upon the trail behind him more often than upon those rocky pinnacles. After the first hour, though, Steve had been fairly confident that there was no pursuit. Probably Galt had seen no point in launching his legion on a hopeless chase. Galt would guess where Steve was heading, and Galt knew the odds that would be stacked against Steve at trail's end. Perhaps Galt, having no other choice, was content to let Steve ride out of one death-trap and into another.

Still, Steve was taking no chances on being recaptured by the Sixty Six-Guns, for he remembered, all too well, the fanatical hatred Spider Galt bore him. He followed an erratic course, seeking rocky ground wherever he could find it, splashing up a shallow stream, utilizing years of accumulated trail-savvy to hide his sign.

As on that night when he'd ridden with the Ox and covered trail from the eyes of the Stormes, he did this work almost mechanically, his mind busy with other things — many of them.

But mostly he dwelt upon the resemblance of his mother's picture to the "ghost lady" of his past. It was uncanny, that resemblance, and the chill of the discovery was still upon Steve. The swift pace of events in Battleweed and beyond, taking him out of one danger and into another, had given him little time to reflect upon the matter but now it crowded his thoughts.

Yet the beginning of madness could come from such thoughts as his, so he probed for a natural solution to the puzzle. There must be such a solution. He couldn't remember seeing the golden locket before. Yet Spider

Galt had admitted stealing it from the Rolling R. Possibly, then, Steve had seen the locket when he was a very small boy. His mother's features might have been etched into his subconscious mind at that time.

Later, on the night when a bullet had made him delerious, he'd been picked up by the wife of one of the small ranchers who'd been driven from the valley. Perhaps she'd been an elderly woman and he'd only retained a fragmentary memory of her, a hazy recollection of gray hair and a lined face. When he'd tried to recall that memory afterwards, he'd subconsciously substituted his mother's features for the face he'd forgotten.

Thus he'd created the "ghost lady" in his mind, the composite of two entirely different women, one of them his mother, one a stranger.

That was it, Steve assured himself. That had to be it. Still, his theory didn't explain the empty coffin at the Rolling R, and Steve couldn't help but wonder if the missing body was some more of the work of Spider Galt. But there was no way of solving the riddle, at least not now. Shrugging, Steve resolutely drove his thoughts to other things. That task was the easier because he was nearing the palisade that barricaded the stronghold of the Stormes.

He brought his purloined field-glasses into play now, sweeping the length of the palisade until he located the huge gate. The last time he'd been here, there had been only one sentry on guard. Now there were four, cowpunchers all of them; two lolling near the gate with rifles in their hands; two, mounted, patrolling the palisade in opposite directions, slowly riding the length of the great fence only to turn back and ride again.

Steve whistled. "Looks like they're mighty ready for visitors," he mused aloud. "The gate's sure enough closed to them that ain't welcome and there isn't much chance of shinnying over the fence, either."

But he hadn't expected to go through the gate — not this time. Darkness had favored him before — and luck. Those four waddies would give a man a hot reception, and discretion was going to be worth a great deal more than valor if an entrance was to be gained.

Refocusing the glasses, Steve swept the palisade from one end to the other. The great fence described an arc, bulging outwardly in its middle. Both ends of the fence flanked the cliffs that backed Storme Castle so that the artificial wall merged with natural walls at either end. There was a rift in the sheer wall of cliffs, a pass of sorts that was the back door to Rearing Horse. But that pass would undoubtedly be barricaded and, besides, to reach it would mean scaling the Bitter Roots to approach it from the far side.

All these factors combined to make a condition that Steve had already taken into consideration. The only means of reaching Storme Castle, other than going through the gate or climbing the guarded palisade — impossibilities, both of them — was to get above the buildings and come down the cliffs. That was why he'd fetched the lariats.

The first chore, though, was to reach the crest of the cliffs. Steve, accordingly, turned his horse to the west and vanished into the timber, toiling up a wooded slope. There was a trail of sorts, but it soon became so steep that Steve had to dismount and lead his laboring horse.

Beyond the timber was a slope that was even steeper, a slope gray with the rubble that dotted it, a sun-washed upward tilting stretch where rattlesnakes probably laired. Steve had to leave his horse behind after he'd burdened himself with the heavy weight of the ropes.

With the hemp coiled around his waist

and loaded upon his shoulders and back, it was effort enough to walk, much less climb. Yet Steve toiled onward and upward, a tiny fly on the rocky face of a mountain. The sun beat down, laying a blistering barrage of heat, and the foggy upper heights seemed as far away as ever.

It was hell's own hike. Perspiration drenched Steve, seeping from under a sombrero he'd picked up in the livery stable, worming down his face, gluing his clothes to him. His face glistened and his eyes stung. When he paused for breath he could look back upon the valley and even see Battleweed glittering in the sunlight, distant and ethereal. And though the season had been dry, the panorama of Rearing Horse looked like paradise to him, an Eden utterly beyond reach.

A dozen times Steve tore his eyes away to resolutely climb onward. The hours tramped by, endless, dragging hours, and thirst came to torture him while hunger left him faint and weak.

It occurred to him that, save for a few berries he'd picked on the lower slope, he hadn't had a bite to eat since yesterday noon when he'd headed for Hop Gow's before the bucking contests. How long ago that seemed!

Far below, Storme Castle sparkled in the sunlight, looking less sinister by day than it had by night, and sometimes Steve made out tiny pigmy figures moving from barn to corral, from outhouse to outhouse.

Steve had long since discarded his glasses, having no further use for them and being glad to be rid of even such a small amount of extra weight. But, peering, he was certain that some of those figures below were women.

Women? They puzzled him at first, until he began to recall that Thunder Storme had a wife, as did his sons, Nahum, Noah and Nathan. Possibly the twins, Theobald and Thaddeus, who were older than their cousin Tom, had also "gone out" to return to the clan with womenfolk later. He recalled, too, that the barkeep in the Buckhorn had mentioned a daughter of Thunder's. And Spider Galt had said that some of the Storme women had come to the rodeo in a buggy, though Steve hadn't seen them.

Steve dismissed the matter. He'd told Sheila that he made no war upon women and he'd meant it. Even the edge of his hatred against Storme men in general had been dulled by the thing he'd learned today. He'd hated all of them, not knowing which one had squeezed the trigger, sending

Dawson Reardon to his grave. But now he knew Thunder Storme was the man he sought and the hatred Steve had borne for all the family was now focused on the ruler of the clan.

Maybe the slate would be wiped clean before another sun rose. Maybe Dawson Reardon could rest peacefully out there on the Rolling R. The thought was enough to goad Steve onward, to unlock some reserve of strength within him that he didn't know existed, to sustain him until he reached the crest of the cliffs, spent and panting, where he lay prone upon the naked rock as long as he dared.

The sun was sloping toward the Bitter Roots as he gained his objective. Dusk was already purpling the valley, the swift dusk of the high country, and there wasn't much daylight left. By dint of Herculean effort, Steve had attained half of his purpose, but the rest of it would be just as hazardous. He had to begin that dizzy descent, straight downward into the very backyard of Storme Castle, and he had to utilize every remaining minute of the dying day.

From the floor of the valley, the cliffs had looked sheer and smooth. But, peering below, Steve saw what he had hoped to see, a series of ledges of sorts and a few rocky protuberances that might aid him.

Uncoiling the first lariat, he looped it around a mammoth boulder that stood sentinel-like, at the cliff's edge. Tossing the rope over the lip of the cliff, he saw that it almost reached the first ledge. Unhesitantly, he wrapped his legs about the rope and slid over the edge, letting himself down hand over hand. At rope's end he had to drop a half-dozen feet, landing cat-like on the narrow shelf of rock.

From here he was able to clamber downward for a considerable distance until he reached another ledge, but further descent proved to be impossible without the aid of a rope, for the cliff dipped inward below this ledge. Exploring the ledge, he found a jutting rock strong enough to support his weight. Uncoiling another lariat and fastening it, he eased out over the edge again, swung pendulum-like for a moment, then lowered himself.

This was a process he was to repeat many times in a slow descent that seemed to take forever. He might have tied all the lariats together into one long rope but if he did that, he'd have no other means of help once he reached the end of that rope. And the rope certainly wouldn't be long enough to reach to the base of the cliffs. He would never have been able to carry such a supply of rope to the crest of the cliffs, even if more lariats had been available — which they hadn't. His plan, then, was to work downward wherever he could, keeping the ropes as a sort of ace-in-the-hole, hoping against hope the while that the worst of the descent would be over before he used his last lariat.

Sometimes luck favored him for once he found a gnarled scrub oak that clung to a crevice, giving him anchorage when he sorely needed it. Sometimes there was nothing at all and he had to toil downward as best he could, his boots tied about his neck, his bleeding hands and feet finding holds in fissure veins, tiny breaks in the wall.

There were moments when terror gripped him as he wondered if he might be stranded here, like a fly pinned to a wall, unable to go either up or down. He fought against his panic, knowing that if he lost his head he would indeed be beaten. But would he ever reach the bottom? He began to wonder if there was a bottom, or if he were doomed to forever work downward into some sort of bottomless abyss.

He was going on nerve alone and he was nearing the breaking point. He'd looked down once and the sight of the yawning depths below him had made his head swim so he'd resolutely kept his eyes elsewhere except when he'd had to gauge the depth of his next descent. Now, with twilight graying the valley, he couldn't even do that and he lowered himself down his last lariat to land in a clump of chokecherry bushes. And it came to him with a start that he'd finished the descent!

Yonder loomed Storme Castle, shapeless and ominous in the gathering gloom. But the daylight had served Steve well and the night was coming to cloak him and the flush of half-a-victory was encouragement enough.

For a long time he lay in the shelter of the bushes, waiting for his heart to cease its wild racing, his chest to quit its tumultuous heaving. Then, donning his boots and locating his sombrero which had fallen near by, Steve stole toward the structures.

There were horses in the corrals, stomping nervously, and riders were loitering about the barn. Any moment someone might challenge him. But to skulk along would be to invite attention by the very suspiciousness of such a procedure, so Steve, nearing the house, strode boldly forward and in this manner he mounted the porch and reached the door of Storme Castle unaccosted.

Now was the moment when he should have remembered that he'd warned Wash Winfield and those other little ranchers that it would be suicide to tackle Storme Castle without a strong force. Now was the moment to turn back if he was ever going to.

But Steve had no intention of turning back, nor did he regret that he'd come alone. For he knew at this moment that his trail was clear before him — had always been. That was why he'd been reluctant to accept an alliance with Spider Galt. He knew it now. That was why he, Steve, had persuaded the little ranchers to delay their fight against the Stormes — though there had been other reasons as well, behind his argument.

Once he'd thought that he wanted allies — but he hadn't, not actually. Scant satisfaction there'd have been in riding to Storme Castle with a hundred helpers at his back! This was his fight, a lone-handed fight, and it had been from the first. Tonight he was alone and that was as it should be. The door yielded to his hand and beyond it he found himself in a great hallway, a mammoth place, thronged with shadows.

It was lamp-lighting time but the lamps hadn't been lighted. Pausing hesitantly, Steve peered into a vast living room, a place of mounted trophies of the hunt and yawning fireplaces. Venturing further inside the room, he found it empty. A spiraling staircase led upward from the hallway and Steve boldly climbed it to find himself in another hallway with doors flanking either side.

He could hear the patter of footsteps in many parts of this great, sprawling house, but there was nothing in the even measure of them to cause him alarm. In this second-story hallway he hesitated only because he was at a loss as to where to proceed.

There was something eerie about the very silence of this building, something that rasped Steve's nerves. He didn't know where to go and he might have begun to try each door, hunting out the throne-room of old Thunder by a process of elimination, but at that moment a woman glided out of a room and headed for the stairway.

She appeared so suddenly as to startle Steve, but there was nothing hostile in her manner and no sign of astonishment in her eyes as they met his. She was middle-aged, Steve guessed, and something in her features vaguely reminded him of the twins, Thaddeus and Theobald. For that reason he presumed her to be Noah Storme's wife and the mother of the pair. He doffed his sombrero, tucking it under his arm.

"Begging your pardon, ma'am," he said, "but I'm looking for Joshua Storme, him they call Thunder. I come from Battleweed with a message for him from Doc Merritt. No one answered when I knocked on the door."

He hated the lie, hated taking advantage of the friendship of Dr. Merritt and these people, but he knew no better excuse for his presence here. Hadn't Doc Merritt said that he, in his professional capacity, was the only outsider who'd ever been admitted to Storme Castle?

Steve waited breathlessly after he spoke, conscious that he must be a very bedraggled figure, alarmed lest this woman had been at the rodeo and would recognize him now, thankful for the cloaking darkness. The woman nodded quickly. "Thunder Storme? His room is to your left at the end of the hall."

He nodded and stalked down the hallway. He risked one backward glance and saw Noah Storme's wife disappearing down the broad staircase. Then Steve was facing the door of the room she'd indicated.

And here he hesitated, finding a strange tremor in his hands yet knowing it wasn't fear that caused it. For fifteen long years he'd awaited this moment. For fifteen long years he'd dreamed of the showdown that lay just beyond this door.

Maybe he'd cross the threshold only once. Maybe he'd been a fool to enter the lion's lair alone. For a moment the sweet face of Sheila floated before him and a picture of all the things that might have been. But he remembered something else as well — the dilapidated building that had once been the Rolling R ranch-house — a grave beyond the weed-choked yard — his own miserable boyhood . . .

So Steve Reardon opened the door of Thunder's room and stepped inside.

It was a big room, a room of draped windows and lengthy shadows, a room filled with old furniture and, likely enough, old memories as well. A long table centered it and at the end of the table, a silent figure sat in a chair, a high-backed chair with carved, ornate arms, an elaborate chair, a throne.

Just for the space of a heartbeat, Steve stood there, his eyes on Thunder's throne, and then the drapes were rustling, a soft, sibilant sound like ghostly voices calling one to another in the gloom. Steve sent his hand darting toward his gun in sudden understanding, but he never finished the gesture. Men were stepping from the concealment of the drapes, five of them, and their leveled guns covered him. They were Noah Storme and Nahum and Nathan and the sons of Noah, Thaddeus and Theobald. Trapped, Steve Reardon slowly raised his hands.

"And keep 'em up!" Noah Storme snapped, his voice echoing in this ghostly room. "We've had you covered right along, Reardon. There were rifles on you as you came down the cliff and you've been under one gun or another since the moment you set foot in this house. But it isn't our way to shoot you down in cold blood as much as you deserve it. You'll get your chance first.

"You see, we managed to trail you after you snatched the Ox from us last night. You covered up well, but we picked up sign — sign that led to the Rolling R. But we got there too late. We found the Ox . . . dead — murdered. You scoffed at Storme law, Reardon. Now you're going to get a taste of it, find out how just it can be. We're trying you for the Ox's murder!"

The very tone Noah Storme used was equivalent to a pronouncement of doom. Yet Steve scarcely heard him. For Steve was staring at the figure on Thunder's throne, staring wide-eyed and slack-jawed. He'd expected to see Thunder sitting there, but this wasn't the white-maned patriarch of the Storme clan. This was a woman, queenly of face, the "ghost lady" from yesteryear.

sixteen

Time might have turned backwards as Steve stood there, staring at the woman on Thunder's throne, seeing that aristocratic face, framed by its halo of graying hair; seeing the years bridged before his unbelieving eyes. It was she. There could be no mistake about it. And while he stared, the woman stirred, raising a bloodless hand, blue-veined, almost transparent.

"Stephen Reardon," she said softly. "You've come back. I knew you would. I've known it . . . ever so long . . ."

Steve, choked and bewildered and awed beyond words, wanted to doff his sombrero. But as he instinctively began the gesture, five gun-barrels flicked in wordless warning.

"I'm — I'm plumb sorry, ma'am," Steve managed to say. "I wasn't expectin' to find you here. It was Thunder I was lookin' for and —"

The transparent hand fluttered again. "I know," she said. "We've known almost every move you've made since you returned to Rearing Horse. We knew who you were seeking when you entered this house tonight. And you might as well hear the truth, at least. It doesn't matter much what you know — now. Joshua Storme, him you call Thunder, passed away . . . three years ago. I am Ophelia Storme, his widow — the head of the house of Storme."

"Thunder — dead!" Steve cried, aghast. "It — it ain't so — !" A sudden suspicion had its way with him. "He's here! He's afraid to face me — just like he was afraid to face me that day the others rode down to Battleweed. He can't be dead. If it was true, some word of it would have leaked out into the valley!"

The face of Ophelia Storme was like a white mask and the only life was in her lips as they moved. "My husband was wounded years ago, wounded the night — the night you left Rearing Horse. He never recovered from that wound. He lingered, almost an invalid, until three years ago when his suffering ended. At my insistence, my children and our employees kept his passing a secret. Only one man outside of Storme Castle knows the truth and that man can be silent as the Bitter Roots when he chooses to be. I am referring to our friend, Dr. Joseph Merritt."

"A secret . . . ?" Steve said, incredulously. "But why — ?"

"So that certain people would believe Thunder Storme to still be alive. In recent years, small ranchers have come back to the valley. We did not oppose their entrance and it is our wish to live in peace with them, for we have learned that peaceful ways are the best ways. But there is a serpent in Battleweed — a slimy, crawling snake who spreads his virus by day and by night. Jasper Galt would bring war to the valley again. Aye, we know his lust for power. But those who believe that Thunder Storme still sits in this chair are hesitant to take up the sword, for they fear Thunder Storme as they fear the wrath of God!"

It was all very amazing, but Steve, listening, found himself beginning to believe. He had to believe and it wasn't entirely the sincerity in her voice that made him do so. He was remembering something Wash Winfield had once said — "Folks has been afraid of their shadders . . . The name o' Thunder Storme is enough to keep a man's gun pouched . . ."

And the more recent words of Spider Galt: "First I figured on riling the small ranchers, getting them to drive out the Stormes . . . The name of Thunder Storme kept them paralyzed . . ."

Such, then, was the power of Thunder

Storme, to live after death, to be an immortal ruling force whose sway extended beyond the grave because this pale shadow of a woman lived a lie and made all of Rearing Horse believe that lie. It was her frail hands alone that were holding the valley from the verge of range war. Her courage was a different sort from gun-courage, but Steve, sensing the strength of it, could respect it the more.

So this was the secret of Doctor Merritt! This was what the old medico had meant when he'd said: ". . . The day you stand before Thunder's throne will be the sorriest day of your life!"

Steve had learned the truth the bitter way. He'd come back to Rearing Horse to wage war upon the Stormes. In waging that war he'd been fighting a woman — a woman who was maintaining a desperate deception for the sake of peace. And this same woman had helped him in the darkest hour of his childhood. Possibly she had been trying, in her own way, to atone for any wrong the clan had done Stephen Reardon. Yet Steve, deeming the score still unsettled, had returned to make war upon her, to increase her troubles twofold.

He bowed his head, feeling the flush of shame and a sense of unworthiness. But he had a sort of lethargic curiosity, too, and he wanted to ask another question — a question concerning a certain golden locket. He *had* to know the answer to that riddle — but the Storme men were surrounding him and the question had to go unasked.

They took Steve's gun away from him and heavy hands forced him into a chair beside the long table. They slowly filed to other chairs. Noah Storme, one hand upon a ponderous leather-bound Bible, the only article that broke the bare expanse of the table, cleared his throat.

"You've been told the truth about our father," he began. "Now we'll get down to the real business. We have our own law here, Reardon, and we try to make it a just law. It is the law that served us well when we had Rearing Horse to ourselves and we've seen no reason to seek outside law to take care of our own affairs. You killed one of our men, the Ox — or so we believe. You're on trial on that account. We don't have a jury or a witness stand or attorneys to do a man's talking for him. The fact is, we don't have much formality of any kind. But it'll be a fair trial and you'll get a chance to speak. So will them that hankers to speak for you — if there be any. Are you ready, prisoner?"

Steve nodded. Once he'd laughed at

Storme law, but tonight there was no laughter in him. This might be some sort of fantastic nightmare, yet the deep solemnity in the voice of Noah Storme was proof enough that the man sincerely believed in what he was doing. Jasper Galt had also accused Steve of the Ox's murder, but that had been part of a farce, a prelude to the *ley de fuga*. This was different. These Stormes actually believed that he, Steve, was a murderer. Their very sincerity was the thing that was spelling Steve's doom.

"Maybe we should have my son up here," Nahum Storme suggested. "When it comes right down to it, he saw more of Reardon than any of the rest of us did. He might have something to say about all this."

"Tom?" Steve asked. "Is he here?"

"He came home last night, kneeing a hoss up the trail, his hands tied behind him. He'd been a prisoner of the Sixty Six-Guns, as you probably darn well know, and he isn't even sure himself just how he managed to escape them. He's in our jailhouse right now."

"In jail!"

"Tom raised a rumpus in Battleweed when he was liquored up and conducted himself in a manner which we do not approve. You jailed him for that, but he only paid part of his penalty. We held a trial for him last night. He's got about two weeks to sit in our jail and reflect on his sins. You've scoffed at Storme law, Reardon. You figgered it was a joke. Maybe now you can understand that Storme law punishes the Stormes any time they need it. You savvy that?"

Steve did. Here was a sort of Roman justice and Steve could not doubt but what this grim clan administered it without fear or favor — especially when one of the twins bobbed out of the room to return some minutes later with a disheveled Tom Storme. The big blond youngster quietly took a chair, his gaze flicking briefly to Steve. Noah Storme took the reins again.

"No need to chaw over what's happened," he said. "All of us except Tom was there. We know Reardon stopped us and took the Ox away on the pretext of arresting him, but refused to name any crime the Ox had committed. We followed him, but we were too hopping mad to have our eyes peeled and he hid out on us. When we did manage to cut sign, it pointed toward the old Rolling R. Reardon, do you mind saying why you took the Ox to your father's old spread?"

"There were things I wanted to find out,"

Steve admitted readily enough. "Things that took place at the Rolling R fifteen years back. The Ox was there that night. I figgered he might be able to remember those things and speak up, once he saw the place."

"The Ox was half-witted," one of the twins snorted. "He couldn't remember things twenty minutes after they happened. Is that how you come to kill him — trying to make him tell you what you wanted to know? That's how it looks, feller. When we burned leather to the Rolling R, he was there alone — dead!"

A murmur rippled the length of the table, an ominous murmur, and Tom came to his feet. Leaning, he wordlessly caressed the Bible for a moment.

"I've got something to say," he announced. "I wasn't in on the doings, so it's opinion rather than evidence that I'm offerin' — but I think it'll make savvy. I knew the Ox. We all knew him. He was touched in the head, a childish sort of a gent. Killin' him would have been plumb easy — as easy as killin' a child, or shootin' a gent in the back . . ."

That was enough to bring a throaty rumble from the Stormes and every face that turned Steve's way was stamped with a scowl.

"But wait!" Tom Storme went on. "We've got to think twice! I reckon I know Reardon, here, better than any of us. Me and Steve Reardon tangled the first night he was in Battleweed. He forced a fight on me, even though I could have given him pounds and had plenty to spare. And he trimmed me, too; but he fought fair. He never used his boots or done any eye-gougin', though there was some present who pointed out that it would be a right good idea to fight dirty . . ."

Tom paused, gestured with one hand. "We tangled again, you might say, in the rodeo arena, and he done some mighty fine riding. It took guts, more guts than most men's got, to stick on Angelmaker. Now here's the way I add them things up — the man that beefed the Ox was a yellow coyote who was doing the same thing as killin' a ten-year-old boy. But you can tell the courage of a gent by the way he fights and the way he rides. I'm sayin' that every step of the way Steve Reardon's proved he ain't the kind of yellow dog that would 'a' put a bullet in a helpless critter like the Ox!"

It was a long speech and there was little doubt but that it impressed the Stormes. Silence lay heavy and solemn after Tom had seated himself, with many minutes trooping by before Nathan Storme lumbered to his feet and touched the Bible.

"There's something to gnaw on in what Tom says," his uncle admitted. "But Tom hasn't got the years some of us has, and he ain't got the savvy that the years bring a man. Maybe he's sized Reardon up right. I sort of think so, myself. But he's forgot that sometimes when a gent is trying to get something, something that he can't quite reach when he wants it mighty bad, the gent loses his temper and does things he'd hate himself for doing if he took time to think. And Tom's forgot that the Ox was a powerful hombre. He was short on brains, was the Ox, but if he took a notion to pile himself on a gent, that man wouldn't have been fighting no child by a darn sight. I'm saying that Tom's speech just isn't no proof one way or another."

Nathan sat down. In the ensuing hush, his brother Noah's questioning eyes ran over the faces of his sons, Nahum, his nephew Tom, flicked to his mother who sat in silence at the far end of the table.

"Stand up, prisoner," Noah Storme said, and when Steve had pulled himself to his feet — "It looks like all the evidence has been presented that's going to be. You want to tell your side of it, Reardon?"

Now was the time for words, but words didn't come to Steve. Now was the time to tell how Spider Galt had gunned for him and later practically confessed to having killed the Ox by mistake. The Stormes would at least listen to such a story. They hated Galt with good cause and knew the man to be capable of any crime. All Steve had to do was to tell them about it.

But would it be worth the effort? Would they believe him after they heard him out? Suddenly Steve knew they wouldn't — and in all honesty he couldn't blame them for the doubt they'd have. He hated the Stormes. Every act of his since he'd returned to Rearing Horse had been inspired by that hatred. They believed him to be vindictive and ruthless because he'd wanted them to believe that way. Now they'd think he was lying to save his neck, to gain a reprieve for himself so he could war against them again.

They'd believe that because he'd already given them reason to believe it. And now, facing his accusers, Steve faced the truth as well. In a minute they'd pronounce judgment on him, sentence him to death. Yet, would it be they who would send him to his doom? No. They were merely the instruments of a destiny that had been fifteen years shaping itself. Steve's own hatred had brought him to this sorry pass.

"I could waste a lot of words," Steve said wearily. "It isn't worth the bother. I've got nothing to say."

Noah Storme arose slowly. "I'd — I'd sorta hoped you'd speak," he said. "You make it harder this way, but I've got no choice." He swung his gaze to his kinfolk. "The Ox was one of us," he continued, "as near to one of the family as any man could be who wasn't related to us. He was a simple gent, but he did his best for us and he counted on us to feed him and protect him and do the things that were beyond his poor addled wits to do for himself. He trusted us and — in the end, we — we failed him . . ."

His voice broke with emotion, but he recovered himself with an effort. "There's nothing left now to do but take the vote — thumbs up or thumbs down. That may be harder for some of us here than for others. But we've all got to remember that it's just one thing Reardon's being tried for — and that's the killing of the Ox.

"We can't let ourselves be prejudiced because we know just why he came back to Rearing Horse. We can't judge him because he sold himself to Jasper Galt, an enemy of every man of us. We can't hold that against him — and we can't let anything else influence us either. The question is whether we're sure, in our hearts, that Reardon killed the Ox. Nahum, are you ready to show your vote?"

Steve bowed his head. He didn't watch as one by one Noah called the roll of the family. He didn't know how each of them voted for he kept his gaze lowered until his own name was called.

"You hate us, Reardon," Noah Storme said slowly. "Perhaps, in your heart, you believe all this to be a farce, our way of murdering you and keeping our consciences clear. Believe me, it isn't so. If one of my own brothers had proved to be guilty, the judgment would be the same — even if I had to pronounce it . . ."

He laid his hand upon the Bible, hesitantly. "We had to be a law unto ourselves when there was no other law. This Book has sorta been our guidance at times when there was nobody to show us the way. Leviticus has something to say about an eye for an eye, a tooth for a tooth You savvy, Reardon? Tomorrow morning . . ."

They were all on their feet, a solemn-faced sextet. Steve caught a last glimpse of Ophelia Storme before they ringed him to shut off the view. She had spoken no word during the trial and she kept silent now. But somehow she looked older, as though this brief hour had piled the years upon her.

Steve shook his head like a dazed fighter. The entire trial here in this room of whispering drapes and crawling shadows, with that ghost-like figure at the far end of the table, had been like a dream to Steve. But now that it was over, it had suddenly become real — as real as the click of a gallow's trap as it is sprung beneath a man's feet, as real as the bite of hangnoose hemp. Then Steve was being hustled into the hallway and down the broad staircase.

A full moon soared above the mountains, painting the cliffs with a phantom's brush, leaving the yard awash with light, as the grim group crossed to a squat log building with barred windows, a queer sort of building with four doors giving into four unconnected rooms, each facing a different point of the compass. They paused before an open door and Tom Storme, turning aside, hesitated.

"Damn it," he said. "I'm sorta sorry about this, Reardon. I still can't quite get a tail-holt on the idea that you beefed the Ox. Will — will you shake?"

Once Steve had decided that hatred would always be a barrier between himself and Tom Storme. But Steve, who had since learned just how poorly hate can serve a man, took the proffered hand.

"I'm thankin' you for what you said upstairs," he muttered. "And — not that it makes any difference now — I'd like you to know it was me who started the fire that sent the Six-Guns stampedin'. It's so-long, Tom."

Without a backward glance, Tom Storme stepped into his cell and somebody snapped a padlock into place. They rounded the building to pause before another open door. Noah Storme pointed into the room beyond.

"We'll be back at sun-up," he announced. "It'll be a gun or a rope then. The choice'll be yours, Reardon."

Steve nodded and the shadowy depth of the jail-building swallowed him. He heard the rasp of the hasp and the click of the padlock. He heard the thud of bootheels as the Stormes marched away and he listened until that sound died in the distance. After that there was silence, deep and enduring as the silence of a grave. . . .

seventeen

It was nearly midnight. The moon had climbed high above the valley and from the barred window of the Stormes' jail Steve had marked the passage of the lengthy hours by watching its slow ascent. In the day-like luminosity he could see the avenue of cottonwoods leading toward the palisade below, a shapeless bunkhouse, sleep-swathed and silent, a jutting wing of Storme Castle. Soon the moon would spend itself and fade away to nothing. Soon there would be darkness, streaked by the first pink heralds of dawn. Then morning would come . . .

The day's doings had exhausted Steve, but sleep refused to claim him. Yet it was not a fear of his impending fate that kept him awake. A sense of futility was upon him, and coupled with it was a sort of fatalism that sustained him. The game had gone against him, but he'd only played the cards as they had fallen. At dawn the deck would be shuffled for the last deal.

Not that Steve was content to be led like a sheep to the slaughter. If there was any chance to escape the doom to which he'd been sentenced, he'd grasp that chance eagerly enough. As soon as the Stormes had left him, he'd examined his cell. This jail-building was constructed sturdily and the room was no more than six feet by six, with a stool and a bunk comprising the furniture. The floor was of dirt, but it might as well have been of stone, for it was hard-packed by the boots of two, possibly three generations of Stormes who had paced this room in repentance. Even the chinking between the logs defied Steve's fingers and after his first survey he'd concluded that the place was escape-proof.

When a grizzled range-cook had appeared shortly afterwards with a plate of food, Steve had eaten it not only because hunger was gnawing at him, but because food would give him strength — strength he might sorely need. But his strength, it seemed, was to avail him little as far as escaping from this cell was concerned.

Steve had no hope of rescue, for who was there to rescue him? And he was not prepared for a miracle, since miracles only happen to those who believe in them. That was why he jerked with surprise when someone fumbled with the padlock outside.

Who was this nocturnal prowler? Steve had seen no one approach the jail-building since the cautious cook had been here, a plate in one hand, a leveled gun in the other. A key grated and the door creaked. Only enemies dwelt here, so only a hostile intruder could be coming. His muscles tensed, Steve crouched to spring, preparing to hurl himself upon whoever stepped across the threshold. And he might have launched himself if the moonlight hadn't outlined his visitor as the door swung open.

It was Ophelia Storme with a heavy shawl thrown over her thin shoulders. She peered into the dark interior, a ring of keys clutched in one blue-veined hand.

"Stephen!" she whispered, and when he moved to her, she held a finger to her lips for silence. Then, just as silently, she extended her hand and he took it, to match her swift, soundless pace across the yard and to the cottonwood corridor that wound downward to the distant gate.

She'd freed him! She had come to his rescue, just as she had come on that long-gone night of gun-flame. Steve asked no questions. The instinct to live was strong enough to make jubilation his only reaction in those first moments of liberation. With the house behind them, she paused in the shadow of the cottonwoods.

"We can talk here," she whispered, and a

forty-five revolver glimmered in the moon-light as she brought it from beneath her shawl and handed it to him. "Later I'll take you through the gate. Guards are on duty, but they'll pass you if I tell them to."

The fierce joy within Steve was sullied by a sudden fear and a feeling of shame at his own selfishness as he took the gun. "But you?" he cried. "I can't savvy why you're doing this for me. But Tom's in that jail-building and maybe he saw you as you crossed the yard. I know the others will be wild, come morning and they find me gone. You'll have to answer to them."

A vagrant moonbeam touched her face and she was more queen-like than ever at that moment. "I am the head of the house of Storme, remember," she said proudly. "I answer to nobody — least of all to my own sons and grandsons. They might stop you, even yet, if they knew about this, but their anger tomorrow will do them no good. You can be out of the valley and beyond their reach by sun-up."

Steve nodded. "Maybe, someday, there'll be a chance to repay you for all this," he said huskily. "I won't be forgettin'. And I ain't forgettin' the other time, either. You see, I still remember the lady with the wagon, the lady who took care of me and loaded me onto the stage the night when I was wounded and alone and the whole darn world had sorta blowed up in my face."

"You owe me nothing for that, Stephen. Do you also remember the Dillon ranch up in the Flathead country, the place where the driver left you? The Dillons were old-time friends of mine — Texas people. But I didn't learn about their death until months after they were buried. I had one of our riders go up there to find you then, but you'd gone and left no trace. I was sorry, Stephen. It wasn't my plan that you should be homeless — ever."

"You meant to keep an eye on me — take care of me all the way through?" he said in vast wonder. "I'm mighty grateful. It sorta wipes the slate clean for Thunder — as clean as it can ever be now."

"You hate the memory of him, don't you?" she said, and shadows were in her eyes. "Please don't, Stephen. Joshua Storme was a queer man, but he was a good one. He was a fighter, yet he hated fighting and tried to avoid it whenever he could —"

"Hated fighting!" Steve echoed, and because she winced he hated himself for the sneer behind his words.

"But he did," she insisted. "He came here from Texas in search of peace, fighting his way across the land of the Kiowas and Co-manches, the Cheyenne and the Sioux. He built Storme Castle and shut himself off from the rest of the world, hoping that by living unto himself, he could live as he chose. But others came. They didn't understand. They thought we Stormes were arrogant, when all we wished was to be left alone. They thought our aloofness was belligerency. Trouble followed — trouble between the small ranchers and ourselves."

"I know," Steve said bitterly.

"But do you? Sometimes the truth does not prove itself until long afterwards. We might have dwelt in peace with the small ranchers and they with us. Rearing Horse was big enough for all, and still is. But the same serpent who spreads his poison today was spreading it then — and for some same selfish reason. Jasper Galt bore false witness, turning neighbor against neighbor, stirring up trouble until hate had blinded all of us to the truth.

"And you may as well know this — you can hate Thunder Storme for rising in his wrath, for bringing the war to the Rolling R, but your father's blood wasn't on his hands. It was Jasper Galt who shot Daw Reardon — Jasper Galt who was pretending to be helping the small ranchers then, just as he is pretending today. The Ox saw him do it and the Ox told me so; long ago when he could still remember!"

"Jasper Galt!" Steve echoed. "I can't believe it! I wish I could — but I can't. You're only saying this to drive the last of the old bitterness out of me. Galt confessed a heap of things to me. He was telling truths because, at the time, he wanted to torture me before he killed me. But he said Thunder did the shooting. Why should he have told the truth about everything else and lied about that?"

She shook her head, the moonlight dancing in her gray hair. "I don't know," she confessed. "But tell me, Stephen; you didn't kill the Ox, did you — even in heat of anger or in self-defense? I don't want to believe that the blood of that poor, witless soul is upon your hands."

"Before God, I didn't!" Steve swore, and then he found himself blurting the story he hadn't told at the trial, telling her of Galt's bragging confession, of the hatred Galt had borne Dawson Reardon and Dawson Reardon's son after him, and of the reason for that hatred. He was finished before he saw that Ophelia Storme was listening in wide-eyed fascination.

"Why didn't you tell this at your trial?"

she demanded. "Why didn't you speak up when you had the chance? Don't you know that my sons would have believed you, even though my grandsons might have doubted the story? We knew the truth! We knew that Jasper Galt hated your father!"

"You knew! I thought you'd believe it was a trumped-up story to save my own hide. I never dreamed —"

"Of course we'd have believed you, Stephen. And I'm going to tell you why. I swore to Thunder that I'd never speak of it, and the others that knew swore silence, too — Noah and Nahum and Nathan and Doc Merritt. Jasper Galt hated your father because your mother chose Daw Reardon instead of him. Galt told you that much of it. Then I'm going to tell you the rest of it — for you've a right to know, oath or no oath. Ruth Reardon, your mother, was my daughter, my baby. Now, Stephen, do you understand?"

Her voice was thick with emotion, but the ring of truth was in it. And Steve, who had learned many astonishing things in the last thirty hours, knew he had learned the most astonishing truth of them all. Now he had the answer to the question he'd never had a chance to ask. At first it left him incoherent, weak with the magnitude of it. At first he could find no words.

"My mother . . ." he said at last. "She was your daughter . . . Then — then you're my grandmother! Nathan and Noah and Nahum are my uncles. And the twins are my cousins, and so is Tom — !"

She smiled at his amazement. "And you are the grandson of Thunder Storme," she reminded him.

His head was whirling, but a lot of things were beginning to make sense. This, then, was the real secret of Doc Merritt, the incredible truth that was to have turned any victory of Steve's into ashes. And the pieces fitted. Now he knew why Ophelia Storme had come to save him when he had been a boy, and come again in this second dark hour of need. Now he knew why his mother's picture had reminded him of his "ghost lady." Scant wonder!

"Come," she said and, taking his hand again, she led him beyond the cottonwood corridor and to a little knoll, not too far distant. Here white headboards glimmered faintly in the moonlight, marking a row of mounds; no more than a half-dozen in all.

"This is our own cemetery," she said, "the graves of those who belonged to us — our kin and riders who died in our service."

There was one mound, shaped more recently than any of them and the flowers that strewed it were still fresh. Steve didn't need to read the headboard to know the Ox rested here. Another headboard bore the name of Joshua Storme, and if Steve had had any last lingering doubt as to whether Thunder rode a greener range, it would have been dispelled by such visual proof. But Steve scarcely saw the patriarch's grave, for his eyes were following the pointed finger of Ophelia Storme, reading the inscription on still another headboard — RUTH STORME, BELOVED DAUGHTER, ADORED SISTER . . .

"Thunder had our riders remove her body the very night after Daw Reardon buried her on the Rolling R," she explained. "That is how she came back home to us. Perhaps, in a way, it was a cruel thing to do, and yet there was no real harm in it; and Dawson suffered none, for he tended that other grave until the day he died, never knowing."

"My mother . . ." Steve said brokenly and cradled his sombrero against his chest.

"My little girl," Ophelia Storme murmured dreamily. "She was just a baby when we came from Texas, Stephen. The only men she ever saw were her father and her brothers and the men who rode for us and

Jasper Galt who'd just come to the valley. But the only one she had eyes for was Daw Reardon. He came to ride for us in those days. He and Ruth sneaked out of the valley and up to Hellsgate and were married. Thunder was furious when he found out, but mostly, I think, because he hadn't been consulted. He liked Daw Reardon then. But when Daw Reardon spoke of starting his own ranch, Thunder drove them both from the castle . . ."

The breeze toyed with her shawl and she shivered. Steve drew her close, his arm about her narrow shoulders.

"Thunder couldn't believe that Ruth would choose to leave all this." The sweep of her hand took in the dark bulk of Storme Castle, the valley beyond where the great herds of the Slashed S grazed.

"She would have been queen here when I passed on, even though her brothers married, for such was the law of the Stormes. Thunder couldn't understand why his daughter chose, instead, a shack with the man she loved. But I am a woman, Stephen, and I understood. Thunder made all of us swear that her name would never be mentioned again. The only outsiders who knew of this thing were Doc Merritt and Galt. When other small ranchers began to settle in the valley, they never guessed that Daw Reardon's wife was a Storme . . .

"Yet things might have worked out to a happier ending. I know Thunder lived to regret his anger. I know he went through hell the night news reached him that you were born and Ruth had — had gone on. He paced the floor till morning, just as Noah is pacing the floor tonight. I heard him awhile ago as I passed his room on my way to you. He and his brothers know that you're of our blood, Stephen, but the Ox was one of us, too, even though he wasn't any kin. Storme law has never compromised with itself. Yet it is hard for Noah, thinking what must happen come morning . . .

"And it was hard for Thunder to go on hating Daw Reardon, especially with you in the picture. Thunder used to send the Ox over to spy on you. The Ox, you see, was fond of Daw Reardon, had been since the days when Dawson rode for us. I know that one day Thunder would have changed the lettering on Ruth's headboard, admitting the truth he couldn't deny to himself, for she was a Reardon, even though Thunder's stubborn heart cried otherwise. And I know that one day Thunder would have ridden to the Rolling R to make his peace with Daw. But that was when cattle began to disappear and Spider Galt spun his web of lies. Soon the small ranchers were lined against the Stormes and Daw Reardon was the leader of the little fellows . . ."

She stirred, smiling through tears. "You must go now," she said gently. "Tomorrow I'll tell them of this, make them see the truth about the death of the Ox. Then, someday, you'll be able to come back to us."

Profoundly moved, Steve took one of her blue-veined hands and kissed it, feeling neither self-conscious nor ashamed of the act.

"I'll stay — now," he said simply. "I've been blind. I didn't even stop to figger it out that Galt deliberately shot the Ox, shot him to keep the big feller from putting the snake-sign on Galt. I've wasted a heap of time hating the very people I should have been helping. There'll be trouble here in the valley. I'd be right proud if my guns could be siding the Stormes."

It was as though the mention of guns had, genie-like, summoned the sounding of guns. Down by the palisade there was a staccato outburst of Colt-thunder, a reverberating volley that shook the silence. Steve spun on his heel, peering into the moon-drenched distance. A half-dozen guns had spoken, almost simultaneously. But now the shroud of silence hung again. Yet something was moving below, down where the fence strung a second fence of shadows. The great gate was swinging inward, slowly. Then it was open and horsemen surged inside.

No need to wonder what had happened to those valiant punchers who had tried in vain to guard the gate. No need to remember the threat of Spider Galt: "The Sixty Six-Guns will strike at the Stormes — and they'll strike hard!"

For the Sixty Six-Guns were pouring through the gateway, thundering up the cottonwood corridor, charging straight for the unguarded door of Storme Castle.

eighteen

Ophelia Storme was the first to find voice. "Run, Stephen!" she cried. "Run, before they see you!"

Steve ran, but before he did he scooped Ophelia Storme into his arms, finding her feather-light, and when he ran he headed toward Storme Castle, the desperate urgency that spurred him giving him added strength, winging his feet. His gun was in his hand, the gun his grandmother had given him, but when he fired, again and again, he didn't take time to aim at those horsemen behind him. He had to arouse the Stormes and the shots would do it.

He risked one backward glance. The Sixty Six-Guns were gaining on them, the drumming hoofs beating louder as the distance narrowed until Steve could recognize Spider Galt and Anse Tarn in the lead. Panting, Steve mounted the porch steps in a single leap and, reaching the door, he fumbled to open it, praying that it would be unlocked.

Lead was smashing about him now, thudding into the heavy portal, ripping splinters from the jamb, plowing furrows in the porch. Then the door gave and Steve almost fell inward. A heavy bar hung vertically on the inside of the door and Steve, depositing Ophelia Storme in the nearest chair, swung the bar into place to barricade the portal.

Storme Castle was in an uproar. Men tumbled down the stairway in various stages of undress. Only Noah Storme was fully clothed, for the man hadn't been to bed. His brothers and sons had hastily tucked their nightgowns inside their trousers. Some were booted and some were barefooted, their boots under their arms, But it was significant that each had taken time to latch a gun-belt about his middle.

Ophelia Storme's hand fluttered. "Galt! He's come! It's happened sooner than we expected. He's already through the gate!"

There was proof enough of that in the thunder of guns out there in the yard, the high and excited yells of the invaders, the spatter of bullets against the walls, the crash of falling shards as a window shattered before that first barrage. The red god was riding again and this time the war had come to the stronghold of the Stormes. Noah Storme, grasping the situation instantly, put himself in charge, bellowing hoarse orders, sending a son to one room, a brother to another. His eyes lighted on Steve.

"Him!" he roared. "What's he doing here?"

"Don't be a fool, Noah!" his mother snapped. "He didn't kill the Ox. And he knows the truth — all of it, for I told him. He just saved my life at the risk of his own. He's here to help us and I'm thinkin' we'll need all the help we can muster. He —"

But Steve was already darting into the vast living room, that place of mounted trophies and yawning fireplaces, to find a station for himself at the side of Thaddeus Storme beneath the shattered window. Once Steve had shot a gun from the hand of Thaddeus, but it was obvious that he had done his cousin no real harm, for Thaddeus was using that hand to trigger efficiently. The son of Noah grunted in surprise as Steve knelt beside him. But Steve's gun, spitting through the window, tumbled a horseman from a saddle, an eloquent announcement of Steve's stand and intent.

Thus the siege began. The Sixty Six-Guns were perfect targets in the brilliant moonlight and the boys in the bunkhouse, aroused now, were buying into this war. Guns were belching from the bunkhouse window, putting the raiders between a raking crossfire. Anse Tarn and Spider Galt recognized the danger of their position simultaneously. Each barked the same order, a command that sent the Sixty Six-Guns from their saddles to the concealment of anything that offered cover. Lead speared from a dozen vantage points.

Noah Storme had also chosen a position in the trophy room and his mother came with him, ignoring her son's startled protests, ignoring his insistent command that she at least stretch herself upon the floor at a place where she would be out of the reach of flying bullets.

"It's liable to be hot and heavy," Noah observed grimly. "We're in a tight. We pinned too much faith in the guards at the gate, figgerin' we'd have a warning and time to be ready. Galt's crew must have injuned up on the guards and cut them down before they had a chance to know what was going on. Discountin' the boys who were on guard and a half-dozen hands down in the valley night-herding, there's only Shorty and Hackamore and three or four others in the bunkhouse, and they're hemmed in, probably. I'd calculate there's between twenty and thirty of those skunks outside — and there's just six of us in this house to really do the fighting!"

"Six of us," Steve repeated slowly, and

then a fear flowed through him to jerk him straight. *"Tom!"* he gasped. "TOM! He's out in the jail-building! If they find him there, all they've got to do is shoot in through the window, shoot him down without a chance in the world for him to defend himself. And Tarn's just the kind of blood-crazy wolf who'd do a thing like that!"

His words paralyzed them all, proving that in the first excitement of the siege, the first rush to defend the castle, not one of them had remembered that Tom was alone and helpless in his prison.

"The keys!" Steve snapped. The ring of keys was still clutched in one of his grandmother's hands and, crossing to her in a bound, Steve snatched them away. "Cover me!" Steve ordered. "Be ready to open the door when I come back. And spread the word around the house meantime, so I don't get cut down by my own family!"

"You're going outside?" Noah Storme bellowed. "You can't do it! It's suicide, man!"

But Steve never heard him, for he was already clambering through the wrecked window to drop lightly to the ground; the keys in one hand, a gun in the other. Suicide, Noah Storme had called it. Perhaps it was suicide, but the die was cast and Steve wondered how many steps he'd take before a bullet leveled him.

How could he possibly rescue Tom Storme? Miracles only happened to those who believed in them — but Steve Reardon had come to believe in miracles this night. And now there was another, for the moon was disappearing behind a cloud, and with the shadow across its face, the yard became cloaked in darkness. For how long? Steve didn't know, but he had to utilize every precious second of that darkness and he did, darting swiftly forward, one eye cocked at that veiling cloud that looked no bigger than his hand.

The moon burst into view again to shed its damning light before he gained the shelter of the squat jail-building. Bullets had been spattering meanwhile, for the Sixty Six-Guns had continued to shoot blindly. Steve sprawled to the ground, no more than six feet from a corner of the jail.

Here he lay, prone and panting, his muscles tensed with the expectation that he'd feel the burn of a bullet any second. But no bullet found him. There were corpses strewing the yard now, mute testimony of the efficiency of Storme marksmanship and yonderly a wounded gunman moaned and cursed. If the Sixty Six-Guns saw Steve sprawled here, they must be mistaking him for one of their own dead.

Inch by inch, Steve bellied toward the building's corner, hugging the ground closely. The distance might have been six miles instead of as many feet. The time that it took to cover that distance might have been measured in years instead of minutes. But at last he reached the corner and the sheltering shadows and he pulled himself to his feet triumphantly. His triumph was short-lived. One shadow was moving among the others — a shadow holding a tilting six-gun. One of Tarn's men had picked this very spot to make his stand!

Steve's own gun tilted, bucking at the same time, and two shots blended with each other so closely spaced as to seem one. Steve felt the burn of fire along his ribs and then he was upon the gunman before the fellow could fire again. Steve's arm raised, came down with dynamite behind it, his gun-barrel cracking the man's skull. Without so much as a moan, the man sank to his knees and pitched forward on his face.

Instantly Steve was fumbling with the keys, trying them in the padlock. The third one fitted and he swung the door inward. "Tom!" he hissed. "Come on!"

Surprise made Tom's voice sound unreal. "Reardon!" he gasped. "You out of your cell? And buckin' the Six-Guns! What's *your* game?"

It hadn't occurred to Steve when he'd planned this mad attempt to save Tom Storme that he might not find the big youngster cooperative. He'd forgotten, had Steve, that there had been developments that Tom knew nothing about — developments that had made Steve an ally of the Stormes. "Come on," Steve pleaded. "If I take time to tell you how I stand, we'll be a pair of dead men. You've got to trust me."

He knew his words were evasive and he waited breathlessly for Tom's reaction. It came in the form of a chuckle, and relief left Steve weak. "Just a minute till I pull on this boot o' mine," Tom whispered. "I've been listening to that damned killer movin' around out there and I lay low with this boot in my fist, hopin' he'd get close enough so I could reach through the bars and let him have it across the head!"

Then Tom was out of the building. Steve, his eyes scanning the heavens, knew he could expect no second miracle. "The best thing to do is to make a run for the house," he decided. "Ready?"

"Ready," Tom said.

Then they were running, darting around the corner of the building and straight across that moon-washed yard where death lay ambushed, running for their very lives. Yonder loomed Storme Castle, looking as big and as old as the mountains — and just about as far away. The distance wasn't great, but death marked every step of it.

The Stormes and the Sixty Six-Guns spied them at the same time, a wild cry of fear bursting from the besieged, a hoarse shout of triumph welling from the enemy ranks. Bullets sleeted about the two and Steve scattered bullets behind him, shooting aimlessly with the hope that he might disconcert the gun-crew long enough to allow Tom and himself to reach safety. But with half the distance covered, the hammer of Steve's gun fell on a spent cartridge and at the same moment Tom clutched at his knee and one leg buckled beneath the big youngster to send him sprawling.

"My leg!" he gritted between clenched teeth. "Run, Reardon! Don't bother about me — I'm out of this race. Git while the gitting's good!"

Steve never hesitated. He stooped and that very act saved his life for a bullet zipped over his head as he grasped one of Tom's arms. Then, with a tremendous tug, he had Tom over his shoulder and, lurching erect again, Steve staggered toward the door.

Once before he'd toted the immense bulk of Tom Storme. Once before he'd carried the blond youngster on his back. He'd been packing Tom down to the Battleweed jail that night as part of a plan to humiliate the house of Storme by humiliating Tom. There was a certain irony in the fact that once again he was carrying Tom Storme, but this time he was doing it to save Tom's life.

Yet there wasn't time to reflect on that. He had to gain that door and he did, for the second time that night, with bullets hammering into the portal even as he reached it. The Stormes were ready and waiting and alert to the needs of the situation. The door swung inward and it was being slammed shut again even as Steve sprawled across the floor beneath the bulk of Tom.

There was a ragged cheer from those who had witnessed the rescue. There were men crowding forward to pound Steve's back and shake his hand, but Steve didn't wait for them. Work still waited for him, gunwork, and he darted back into the trophy room at once, to resume his place beside Thaddeus Storme who was still triggering methodically, so busy at his task that he only spared time to give Steve a congratulatory grin.

After that the siege dragged on, becoming a matter of firing — loading — lining sights on elusive, shadowy targets — firing — loading . . . Steve hankered to catch Spider Galt in his sights, but the bony man was far too cautious to expose himself, even for a minute. He was back in the shadows somewhere, goading his hirelings, urging them on to greater fury.

"It's gettin' to be mighty hot," Steve muttered, and his gun clicked empty again. Instinctively he fumbled at his waist, remembered that he wore no gun belt and groped in his pocket for the last of the cartridges he'd taken from Battleweed the morning before. Somebody thrust a handful of bullets to him and he was surprised to find that a woman had anticipated his needs, supplied him and darted away.

There were four women in the castle besides Ophelia Storme, he discovered. They flitted from room to room, helping as best they could. One was the wife of Noah Storme, whom Steve had met in the upper hallway last evening. Another, a woman of about the same age, Steve guessed to be Nahum's wife, Tom's mother. There were two younger women, the wives of the twins obviously; sweet-faced ranch-girls who had chosen to follow Thaddeus and Theobald from some distant range to this lonely valley.

Time paced to the tune of thudding bullets. The bulk of the raiders were concentrated before the house, a strategic spot since they were safe from bunkhouse bullets yet could keep the Storme punchers from joining the house defenders. Soon most of the Stormes were in the trophy room, siding Steve and Thaddeus. Tom was among them, his leg hastily bandaged.

There was no time for talk among them. There was only time for that endless routine of loading, picking a shadowy target and firing. Ophelia Storme was doing her part too. Steve had seen her in many roles — queen, mother, woman. Now he saw her as a fighter, and the spectacle of those blue-veined hands cramming shells into a hot rifle and passing the weapon to a son or grandson was inspiring.

It gave Steve a strange sort of thrill, an awakening, as though now he actually realized the truth for the first time. This valiant clan was *his* clan. These were his people! In blindness he'd fought them, joined a common enemy against them. Now the fates had given him a chance to atone for his errors. He, too, was a Storme, even though his name was different. Now he knew why he'd unhesitatingly braved the dangers of the yard to rescue Tom. Now he knew he'd fight beside the Stormes to the flaming finish.

But they were beaten. No Storme admitted it, but the passing hours made the truth undeniable. They were taking toll, for men screamed and cursed out there in the shadows, then cursed no more. Men reared into view to pitch forward on their faces. But the end was only a matter of time. Noah Storme, his ruddy face pasty, his gun-arm hanging bloody and useless at his side, summed up the situation during the first long lull in the firing.

"They've got our forces split three ways," he said grimly. "The boys in the bunkhouse can't reach us and we can't reach them. And with those skunks inside the palisade, all they've gotta do is swing the gate shut again and post a few men at the fence and they can keep the night-herders from joinin' us if they've heard the gunfire and are honin' to take a hand."

"But we've got the house!" Steve pointed out hopefully. "We've got walls to keep most of the bullets from us. Maybe we'll wear them galoots down in time."

"Likely it will be the other way around," Nathan Storme observed drily. "They can reach the wells and the reservoir for water. And two or three of 'em can sneak off for grub and ammunition if they need it. Sooner or later we're going to run out of all three things. But I reckon we can cross that bridge when we come to it. Like you say, Stephen, we've got the house and it's a mighty good advantage. Maybe —"

He paused, his nose wrinkling and a fear widening his eyes. And that was the moment when every one of them became aware of the thing Nathan Storme had just sensed, the factor that made the stronghold no protection at all and by that token put an end to their one last hope.

"Smoke!" Nathan exclaimed. "So that's why they quit shooting for a while! They've fired the house! Do you see what it means? They're going to burn us out of the house —, and pick us off the minute we show our faces outside!"

nineteen

Storme Castle had been fired! There could be no doubt about it. Somewhere, possibly at the outer wall of one of the wings, the torch had been applied and already smoke tendrils had wormed their way to the trophy room to coil across the floor, writhing like shadowy snakes. The clan was doomed and beneath the heavy hand of this disaster they stood in a sort of stricken silence. Steve was the first among them to find his tongue.

"It's the sort of trick that Spider Galt would think up!" he said bitterly. "It's the one thing that will lay us right in their laps."

"I'm not so sure," Theobald countered grimly. "It's a big house. It'll be a long time burning. We'll show 'em! We'll move from room to room, keeping one jump ahead of the flames. We'll make a stand to the last ditch. Spider Galt will find out that the Stormes sell mighty high!"

Steve peered through the window, bobbing out of harm's way before a questing bullet came buzzing.

"There's about an hour of moonlight left," he guessed. "The dark before dawn will be coming pronto and we could maybe make a dash then. But by that time the house will be a blazing torch lighting things up like daytime. And they'll be expectin' us to hold out till the last minute. Folks, do you see this thing the way I see it? Our big chance is to make a dash *now!* We haven't got more'n the ghost of a chance — but we won't have that if we wait!"

His piece spoken, he looked from one tight-lipped face to another. He saw jaws tighten with determination and eyes narrow with thought. He saw uncertainty and deliberation take their hesitant course. But he also saw them nod slowly, one by one, as they thought it over.

"The boy's right — dead right!" Noah Storme announced for all of them. "We've got to chance it. The men will go first, the women behind them. The sooner we do it, the better. You folks ready?"

The house of Storme had made its decision and there was no further need for words. There was a moment when men looked to their guns. There was a moment when men squeezed their wives' hands with an assurance that none of them could have possibly felt. Then, while time seemed to stand still, the family was massing behind the heavy door.

It was a desperate attempt they were about to make and even Steve, who had suggested it, knew the chances were mighty slim that any of them would reach safety. True, Steve had succeeded in getting from the house to the jail-building and back again, but luck had favored him. Lone-handed, he'd been much less conspicuous than this group was going to be. Besides, the Sixty Six-Guns hadn't been expecting his attempt but the chances were that they were already on guard against a general exodus from the doomed house.

For a moment Steve toyed with the notion of speaking up and calling off this whole play. He could volunteer to make another single-handed attempt to leave the castle. Perhaps he could even get beyond the palisade and into the valley and arouse the small ranchers. Those little cattlemen had already begun to suspect that it was the Sixty Six-Guns who were their enemies, rather than the Stormes. Once they were told the whole truth, they'd be willing to ride to the rescue of the beleaguered castle.

But even as he turned the idea over in his mind, Steve knew it was based on a futile hope. Granting that he'd be able to escape from the castle, a dubious possibility, it would take hours to gather a sufficient force of the small ranchers to save the Stormes. There weren't hours to spare. There weren't even minutes to squander any longer. It was now or never, and their only chance was to go through the door — all of them.

Steve and the twins were in the lead, Nahum and Nathan flanking them. In spite of his protests, Noah Storme, his gun-arm useless, was pushed to the rear where the women huddled. So was Tom, hobbling along on his wounded leg. Steve swung back the bar, wrenched the door open. "Here goes!" he said, and then the group was charging across the porch and down the steps into the yard, their guns exploding.

This desperate strategy had at least given the Stormes the advantage of surprise, for it was patent from the first that the Six-Guns hadn't expected them to make a break quite so soon. For one breathless minute there in the moonlight there was no one to challenge them. Then guns were spitting fire and boots were thudding against the packed earth as the Sixty Six-Guns surged forward, a deadly wave to engulf the Stormes.

At Steve's side, Thaddeus Storme groaned and clutched at his hip. A bullet seared Steve's shoulder but Steve scarcely felt it. Before him loomed the gorilla-like shape of Anse Tarn and there was a savage grimace on the gunhog's red face. Steve, thumbing his gun, shot Anse Tarn between the eyes. The man raised clenched, beefy fists to the sky and dropped and Steve, hurdling his dead body, charged onward relentlessly.

The leader of the wolf-pack was down, but the passing of Anse Tarn only aroused his followers to greater fury. They came now, an avenging horde, their guns poised for a barrage that would beat the Storme clan to the earth, level every last one of them as Thaddeus was already leveled, wounded and out of the fight. This was the finish and Steve knew it. He might work his gun until it was empty but the end was inevitable. Yet knowing this, he felt no fear, for he was sustained by a detached sort of feeling, as though he were a remote spectator seeing this last fight from afar. Triggering automatically, he dashed straight ahead.

But there were things Steve couldn't understand and the mystery behind them sliced through his hazy consciousness. Noah Storme had guessed there were between twenty and thirty raiders. Why should there be over fifty men in his yard? Why were some of them mounted and some afoot? It didn't make sense to Steve. But the crowning wonder of it all was that some of the raiders were turning their guns against the others!

Steve shook his head as though to shake away the unbelievable things he was seeing. Hell, that was Wash Winfield on a rearing horse, triggering toward a scurrying gun-hand! And that was Doc Merritt with a smoking six-shooter in his fist! And those others — Steve had seen them before — Link Telford with his arm in a sling and Gar Mason and the rest of the small ranchers from the lower valley!

Then Steve understood and a wild cowboy yell burst from him. Help had come! The small ranchers were here, led by Wash Winfield and Doc Merritt, turning upon the gun-crew who had persecuted them so long, taking their revenge for burned barns and cut fences and all the thousand miseries that had been heaped upon them. The small ranchers were siding the Stormes, making the yard into a shambles, routing the remnants of Anse Tarn's wolf-pack, sending them in wild, disordered retreat!

All that Steve saw and he saw something else as well, something that spurred him into instant action. Spider Galt, his bony face fear-contorted, was mounted now and he was whirling his horse, deserting his defeated forces. Spider Galt was breaking away. Near Steve a riderless horse reared in panic, its reins trailing. Instantly Steve was into the saddle. And when Spider Galt sank steel into his cayuse and headed down the cottonwood corridor toward the palisade, Steve thundered after him.

The great gate was wide open. If, as Noah Storme had feared, the Sixty Six-Guns had posted sentries here, those guards must have received the same hot-lead treatment from the little ranchers as the Six-Guns had meted out to the loyal cowboys the Stormes had posted at this place. Certainly only huddled dead men were at the gate and Spider Galt galloped through and away unchallenged. But after him came Steve, his body bent low over the saddle horn, his spurs raking the borrowed cayuse's flanks.

He'd pursued Spider Galt in this manner once before; the time he'd tried to catch Galt after the murder of the Ox. Galt had escaped then. But Galt wouldn't escape now, Steve promised himself grimly. Loading as he roared along, Steve had his gun in readiness, but he held his fire, concentrating on keeping that horseman ahead of him in sight. He hadn't forgotten that Galt knew this country far better than he did. He wasn't making the mistake he'd made that other night.

Down past the great herds of the Slashed S, Galt rode, forcing speed from his mount as though hell itself bayed at his heels. On and on he went, with the valley broadening as the miles blurred past. And down through the valley Steve rode after him, clinging to the trail as tenaciously as a tick, never gaining, never losing ground. Try as he might to squeeze more speed out of his mount, Steve couldn't shorten the distance between himself and Galt. But at least Galt wasn't gaining and there was satisfaction enough in that. So long as horseflesh endured, Steve Reardon would be on the trail.

Galt had recognized him. The man had thrown several startled glances over his shoulder and his bony face twitched with terror. Moonlight danced on his gun-barrel as he sent lead screaming backward, but Steve was an uncertain target. Even when those bullets zinged ominously close, Steve held his own fire, content to cling Indian-fashion to the side of his horse while death pelted about him. There would be a time for shooting, but that time was yet to come.

And so the deadly race dragged itself out in the last light of the dying moon. Galt ceased trying to shoot Steve out of his saddle. Galt was bent over his own horse now, intent on outdistancing his pursuer, and it became a savage, silent race — hunter and quarry roaring across the face of a lonely, deserted world. Steve heard no sound but the thunder of hoofs, the scream of the wind past his ears. He guessed that Galt was heading for Battleweed, since the man was beelining in that direction. But Galt abruptly veered from the trail, heading for the shapeless bulk of the foothills.

Spider Galt was going to try and shake off his pursuer in those tangled hills! Steve sensed the man's purpose almost instantly, but the realization only served to tighten his jaw and strengthen his determination not to be eluded this time. Galt's horse was faltering. Inch by inch Steve was gaining, closing that distance between them. But the race was far from run and Galt was still beyond his reach when the trail took them into country that looked familiar to Steve.

And then, almost with a start, he recognized the little bluff yonderly, that cottonwood with the faded headboards beneath it, that ramshackle house and barn and the corrals so desolate and deserted, for this was the Rolling R.

He was never to know why Galt had headed here. Perhaps the man, realizing that his horse was almost spent, had wanted to get into timbered country where the race would go to the wily rather than to the fleet. Or perhaps he'd entertained some notion of putting himself behind walls to pick off Steve as he rode by. Now Steve raised his gun and fired.

His intent was to try and stun Galt's horse by laying a bullet between its ears as a professional horse-hunter creases the cayuse he seeks to capture. It was an impossible shot under the circumstances, for Galt's body was in the way and Steve didn't want Galt to die — yet. The lead burned the mount's flank and it reared so suddenly as to spill Galt from the saddle. The man sprawled on the ground, but only for an instant. Coming to his feet, he clawed frantically, trying to grasp the flying reins as the bullet-scorched horse plunged about wildly, then bolted into the shadows. With a hoarse cry of fear, the bony man ran blindly, but the futility of flight must have struck him. At the Rolling R ranch-house he paused, flattening himself against the wall and jamming shells into his forty-five.

Steve was out of his own saddle at once, stalking forward as relentlessly as doom. Ten paces from Galt he paused, his legs planted apart.

"Tell me, Galt," he asked almost conversationally, "why did you lie about Thunder? Why did you tell me he killed my dad? All the other pieces have fitted into the puzzle but that one."

"I aimed to make you squirm some more," Galt spat defiantly. "I didn't finish the things I had to say to you in Battleweed's jail yesterday morning. Just before I fixed things so you'd walk out into a bullet, I was going to tell you that you were a Storme. I was saving that till the last. I wanted you to die believing that Thunder, your own grandfather, had killed your dad."

"I see," Steve said and nodded. "It happens that I know who really did that killing. You've got a gun, Galt. Why don't you use it?"

And Galt did. With a wild cry of hatred and despair, he raised his forty-five and fired. Steve didn't move. A bullet buzzed by his ear and another plucked at his sleeve as Galt, fear-crazed and shooting blindly, wildly, fired again and again, shot with a desperation that defeated its own purpose. Then Steve slowly, deliberately, leveled his own gun and squeezed the trigger.

He wasn't conscious of aiming. And he didn't wait while Galt quivered and choked, bending at the middle and seeming to hang there as though impaled by an invisible spear before he crumpled, slumping forward. Steve had known what his bullet would do. How could he miss when he'd waited fifteen years to fire that bullet? Nor did he take time to reflect that there was a certain ironic justice because Galt was dying on the very spot where he'd murdered Dawson Reardon. Steve was into the saddle and galloping back toward Storme Castle even as Galt gasped out his life.

There was a semblance of order in the vast, corpse-studded yard when Steve reached it in the first pale flush of dawn. A bucket-brigade had been formed between the reservoir and the house and the Stormes and small ranchers alike were working and had almost extinguished the blazing wing of the castle. Steve sought out Doc Merritt, finding the cherub-faced medico coatless, sweating with the others.

"I learned the secret you hinted at," Steve began. "I've come here to say you were right when I was too stubborn to listen. And Sheila was right, too, when she said hate could eat inward at a man. Tell her —"

"Tell her yourself!" Doc Merritt roared. "She'd be up here now if she knew what was going on. As it is, she's home crying her eyes out because she doesn't know what fool risk you might happen to be running. Son, I'm thinking you left some unfinished business in Battleweed. Was I you, I'd be riding!"

twenty

But many things were to come to pass before Steve saw Sheila again. The fire had to be extinguished, but that was done before the dawn lined the eastern peaks in a glory of gold and scarlet, the gunmen who remained alive being pressed into bucket-brigade service under the alert guns of their captors. Then there was time to snatch a few hours of badly needed sleep. Doc Merritt was at Steve's bedside when he awoke, and the two found much to talk about.

"You can thank Sheila — and yourself — for the help that came last night," Doc explained. "When you told her about Jasper Galt's plan to dominate the valley, she came home and told me about it. I took no sides when trouble came before and I didn't figure on taking sides this time. But damn it, the first thing I knew, I was telling Wash Winfield all about it."

He shook his silvery mane ruefully. "We rode down into the lower valley, the two of us. We talked to the ranchers and we found most of them pretty eager to listen. They'd been doing quite a bit of thinking since Galt had faced his cards and shown that the Sixty Six-Guns were his men. The fact that the Six-Guns had taken over Battleweed didn't set so good, either. When we said it sure looked like Steve Reardon was going to be in a tight, bucking that whole crew alone, the boys began to dig guns out from under their mattresses.

"We started looking for Tarn's bunch and the pack of them had cleared out of Battleweed. The sign pointed straight to Storme Castle. I thought the cowmen might buck at siding the Stormes, but I guess most of them had stopped to figure that when it come right down to it, they didn't have a thing against the Stormes."

He paused, laying an affectionate hand on Steve's arm. "I'm glad you finally learned my secret," Doc said. "I'd have broken my vow and told you myself if I'd thought it would have stopped you. But every man has two loyalties — to his mother and to his father. I wasn't sure but what you'd still hate the Stormes for what happened at the Rolling R, even if you learned you were kin to the Stormes yourself. You see, I knew that much and I knew there was one empty coffin at the Rolling R, but I didn't know until this morning that it was Galt who had done for your father. Ophelia Storme told me when we were comparing notes."

He came to his feet ponderously and fumbled for his hat. "Now I'll be riding, son," he said. "I didn't dast tell Sheila what was up. I know the folks here will want to have a chance to talk things over with you. Tell you what! I'll let Sheila know you're safe and sound, tell her you'll be loping to Battleweed quick as you can . . ."

And the Stormes were waiting a chance to talk to Steve. He sat in their council when they decided what was to be done with the remainder of the Sixty Six-Guns, sat at the same long table in the same shadowy throne-room where not very many hours before he'd been on trial for his life. There was much discussion of the problem before them, but Ophelia Storme reached a decision for the clan.

"There's been bloodshed enough," she said wearily. "We'll give them horses, head them out of the valley. There's too few of them left for them to ever be a menace to anybody. The Sixty Six-Guns are gone forever."

Then there was time for the Stormes to shake Steve's hand, to accept him as their kin. The sons of Thunder had known the truth all along, of course, and the third generation accepted it readily, and, in the case of Tom who had been paroled from the jailhouse, enthusiastically. He pounded Steve's back.

"And you're my cousin!" Tom chortled. "I should have known it. I should have known it by the way you slung your fists and by the way you stuck a saddle. And I should have known it by the cussed, ornery stubbornness of you, which same you couldn't have gotten from anybody else but old Thunder himself!"

"You do a pretty fair job of slingin' fists and stickin' a saddle yourself," Steve grinned, but a crowding thought erased his grin. "There's something I've had a mind to ask you to do, Tom," he said soberly. "It was to be best man at a wedding but — but . . . Aw, hell! Seein' as how you and Sheila —"

Tom laughed, his big blond head tilted backwards. "Feller, you can count me in on that chore right now — and likewise for a piece of the weddin' cake. Shucks, man, me and Sheila was never more'n friends, even though there was some talk of me askin' her to marry me. You see, it was Thunder's hope that the Stormes and the Merritts would join up someday. Since I was the only single feller when Sheila come of age, it sorta made me elected. But this way Thunder will have got his wish and everybody concerned will be a heap more satisfied, I reckon . . ."

Afterwards Ophelia Storme had words with Steve alone, and the grandmother and grandson talked most of the afternoon away.

"It's a happy day, Stephen," the old lady said. "I want to preserve the happiness and the peace of it. Look out yonder window and you'll see the ranchers mingling with my children, all of them talking like old friends. It makes me wonder if Thunder's way wasn't the wrong way.

"The railroad is coming, you tell me. It means prosperity for the ranchers, even those who got into the grasp of Jasper Galt, for I'm thinking that any mortgages of Galt's will molder with him. It means the end of the past and the beginning of a new day.

"Perhaps it will be best to divide the Storme holdings, let each of my children have his own place. Perhaps if we began to live like the small ranchers, they'd come to feel we were their kind of people. For myself, I want no more than to be here the rest of my days, near to Joshua. Surely Storme Castle will never symbolize might to the little people if only a lonely old woman dwells here. And your plans, Stephen? What are they?"

"The Rolling R is mine, legally and by any right," he said. "It could be restored easily enough, and there is room for another cattleman in the valley. I'd like to think that you'll be there often, and the others, too."

And later, when Steve rode down toward Battleweed at the close of the day, he remembered what else he'd said to his grandmother. "It'll be like really coming home at last. It'll be making up for those lost years."

But Sheila would be part of any plan he would ever make from now on. That was why the miles seemed endless and he fretted to sight the false fronts of the town.

And thus it was that Steve Reardon came to Battleweed again. He left his horse at the livery stable and stoop-shouldered Ernie Ide took his meticulous orders concerning oats and water. But Ernie Ide listened with no great interest, for Ernie was old and his eyes were dim and the thing that lighted Steve's face was beyond his understanding.

Crossing the street, Steve passed Hop Gow's eating place without so much as a sideward glance, for the hunger within him this night was not for food. Yet it was like that other night as Steve headed toward Merritt's cottage, for now the moon was aloft again, spraying its same silvery mist through the same tree tops, tracing the same lacy pattern across the ground.

And once again he came at last to the white, vine-covered, flower-fringed cottage and the fence that bore the nameplate of Dr. Joseph Merritt and the whole of it was like something from a picture book. But there was no loneliness within Steve as he saw the light glowing in its windows and the smoke eddying from the chimney. Instead he knew an abiding satisfaction as he fumbled with the latch, admitted himself, and walked up the flagstone path to the porch and raised the ancient iron knocker.

It had come to him now that this was different from that other night he recalled and a strange happiness filled him because it was different. He was rid of all his hatred, purged of all the bitterness that had bound him, just as this valley that now belonged to the valiant was purged of the evil that had so long contaminated it. He was Steve Reardon — a free man . . . free to take the girl he loved into his arms . . . free to face his true destiny at last.

He heard the whisper of footsteps, saw the door open. Then *she* was there. And in her white dress she was like a white flame in the doorway as she stood there with her arms outstretched, smiling . . . waiting . . .

We hope you have enjoyed this Large Print book. Other Thorndike Press or Chivers Press Large Print books are available at your library or directly from the publishers.

For more information about current and upcoming titles, please call or write, without obligation, to:

Thorndike Press
P.O. Box 159
Thorndike, Maine 04986 USA
Tel. (800) 257-5157

OR

Chivers Press Limited
Windsor Bridge Road
Bath BA2 3AX
England
Tel. (0225) 335336

All our Large Print titles are designed for easy reading, and all our books are made to last.